LEADVILLE AVENGERS

Leadville was the hottest, wildest mining town in the West, where fortunes in silver were made in a day and death came cheap in the night.

When a cutthroat gang seized the town by force, the Rio Kid gathered forces of vengeance for a deadly showdown—and the streets of Leadville turned into a river of blood!

LEADVILLE AVENGERS

Tom Curry

GUNSMOKE

This hardback edition 2008
by BBC Audiobooks Ltd
by arrangement with
Golden West Literary Agency

ISBN 978 1 405 68196 4

British Library Cataloguing in Publication Data available.

Printed and bound in Great Britain by
Antony Rowe Ltd., Chippenham, Wiltshire

BT

CHAPTER I

"Pike's Peak or Bust"

☐ Bob Pryor, known on the wild Frontier as the Rio Kid, carefully descended the steep rock slide, carrying on one powerful shoulder the tender joint of mountain sheep carved from the animal he had shot.

The elusive creatures, leaping from crag to crag with their marvelous agility, were difficult targets, which was what made it such sport. With two companions, the Rio Kid had come to the Rocky Mountains, to Colorado, for the unequaled hunting the wilderness offered—mountain sheep, grizzly bear, beaver and other game whose pelts were valuable in the market.

But the financial side was secondary on this trip. The Rio Kid was a restless wanderer through Western danger trails and required change and new scenes. This place was satisfying to his soul.

Not so many years had elapsed since it had been "Captain Robert Pryor, U. S. A." He had fought through the Civil War under Generals Sheridan and Custer and shone as a scout and soldier.

In the clothing he wore now were reminders of the days when he had known only military life. His hat was a campaign felt, with the brim narrower than the usual Western Stetson and his blue pants were tucked into expensive Army boots with silver Army spurs. A blue shirt, bandanna, and Army Colts in the holsters of his cartridge belts completed his attire.

His eyes were blue with a devil-may-care glint that showed the reckless courage of his kind. His nose was straight, his chestnut hair crisp, and his smooth bronzed cheeks were glowing with health. A certain lithe way he moved showed his strength, though he was in no sense burly. Rather, he was the ideal height and weight for a cavalryman—not too heavy, but broad of shoulders, and with a wiry body that tapered to narrow hips.

Although the Rio Kid had been born on the Rio Grande, in Texas, he had gone with the Union during the Civil War. After it was all over, finding his parents dead and his boyhood home destroyed, he had been seized by wanderlust and had kept moving. Since then, his home had been wherever he chanced to be. The prairie, the desert, the mountains, the wild cowtowns of Kansas and the whole Southwest knew him.

He was whistling under his breath now, puffing a bit, for at the 11,000-foot altitude the air was rare.

Swinging past some scrub brush, he could look down on the little park where the hunters had left their horses. Suddenly he checked his progress, staring, as he saw a man picking up the reins of a buckskin gelding. That bucksin, rejoicing in the name of Houston, belonged to Bat Masterson, one of the Rio Kid's comrades. Bat and Celestino Mireles, a Mexican youth who was the Rio Kid's closest friend and constant companion were with him on this hunting trip. They had gone over to the other spur.

It was neither Masterson nor Mireles down there with the horses now. The Rio Kid dropped his meat and grabbed the rifle from its sling on his back. But it was a long shot and as yet he was not sure of the intentions of the fellow with the horses.

He hurried on down toward the park. As he neared he saw the man mount the buckskin, swing around and ride over to catch the mouse-colored dun which was grazing nearby.

That was too much for Bob Pryor, for that dun was Saber, the Rio Kid's own horse that had gone through the war with him. Rangy, and sporting a mirled eye and a mean temper with anyone except Pryor and his friends, Saber was not the sort of animal to be easily approached. He moved away now as the man on the buckskin tried to seize his reins. And then, as the rider followed, he suddenly bit at the reaching hand and lashed out with his hoofs, kicking the buckskin in the ribs.

Bat Masterson's mustang reared high, and bucked violently. He threw the man who meant to steal him off his back, then stood placidly where he was, quieting at once.

The Rio Kid was rapidly moving closer. As the infuriated stranger below jumped up, only bruised by his fall, Pryor knew now that he had come upon a horse-thief—just in time. He threw his big-game rifle to shoulder and placed a shot close over the head of the man.

The whine of the heavy bullet and the echoing report panicked the horse-thief. He raced for the buckskin and leaped aboard. Low over the horse's neck, he drummed his heels against Houston's ribs.

The Rio Kid was near the level ground of the park now, and shrill blasts whistled from his puckered lips. It was an old Army song, and always on hearing it, the dun would come running.

It was as if the warhorse knew the words:

> Said the Big Black Charger to the
>   Little White mare,
> "The Sergeant claims yore feed bill
>   really ain't fair."
> Said the Little White Mare to the
>   Big Black Charger,
> "That Pinto Stallion whispered that
>   he'd like his harem larger!"

Upon hearing this now, Saber threw up his head,

7

shook his mane, darker in hue than his coat, and with tail flying galloped to the Rio Kid. Leaping to saddle, Pryor tore after the fellow riding Houston. He could quickly see that the man was a poor rider, and did not know how to handle the half-wild mustang breed of the Frontier. Rapidly he came up, and drawing a Colt—he had thrown down his heavy rifle when he had leaped to Saber's back —the Rio Kid began firing over the thief's head.

He aimed high, not from any consideration for the horse-thief, but because he did not want to injure Masterson's mount. After a couple of close ones, the bearded, ragged rider ahead lost his nerve. The Rio Kid, gun raised, could see his frightened eyes as he glanced back over his shoulder and found Pryor grimly overtaking him.

Suddenly the horse-thief threw up his hands and Houston slowed. The man tumbled off and lay in the bunch-grass, as the Rio Kid tore up, pistol ready.

"Don't shoot me—please, Mister—don't shoot me!" the fellow pleaded, utter and abject fear in his quavering voice. He was shaking all over.

He wore dirty, torn overalls and shirt, and his head with its long, matted sandy hair was bare. His face was dirt-stained and with beard stubble on the thin cheeks. He was tall and gawky, with washed-out gray eyes and a weak chin. All in all, the Rio Kid didn't fancy the appearance of this scared horse-thief.

"Stand up, cuss yuh!" Bob Pryor snarled.

Plainly the man knew the penalty for stealing a horse in this Western country, and believed that instant death was staring him in the face.

"No—no, don't—don't kill me!" he wailed.

"Get up and lemme see yuh," ordered Pryor.

The man at last obeyed. He was scared silly, thought Pryor, with disgust, as the thief got to his feet shakily, begging abjectly for life. His knees would scarcely hold him, and he was fishy white under his coating of suntan. His lips trembled and he was sobbing, his tears flowing freely, streaking his gaunt, dirty face.

He had a pistol hidden under his shirt, which the Rio Kid quickly discovered and confiscated. He also had a small bundle of food, and some money.

"I ought to string yuh up," growled Pryor angrily. "No hoss-thief deserves any—"

Then the Rio Kid heard a far-off hail. It came from a ridge ahead. It wasn't his friends calling, for they were behind him.

Several men afoot appeared on the ridge, trudging along. They waved to him.

"Those friends of yores?" demanded Pryor of his captive, on guard after what had occurred.

The fellow looked around, and nodded.

"Yeah, from the wagon train."

"What train? And what's yore handle?"

"They call me Turkey—Turkey Craw." With the thin, scrawny neck, and huge Adam's apple that horse-thief had it was easy to see where he got his nickname. "Them folks are some of the boys. We was up to Pike's Peak."

"Are they all like you?" demanded the Rio Kid sarcastically.

"Turkey" Craw sniffled, and did not seem to be too glad to see the men who were coming down the ridge side. In the lead was a long-limbed, tall young fellow wearing corduroys, a miner's hat, and high-laced boots.

Ready for trouble, the Rio Kid waited for the group. The young man ahead stopped, staring curiously first at Pryor, then at Turkey Craw.

"Howdy, Mister," he said to the Rio Kid and his voice was pleasant. "My name's Harris Evers. I'm a prospector. Travelin' with a wagon-train. We're camped across the ridge there."

He had good eyes, hazel in color, an easy-going smile, and a bronzed face that was clean-shaven save for an incipient mustache. The Rio Kid liked the man's looks as well as he liked his voice:

"Is this scum one of yore party?" asked the Rio Kid, indicating Turkey.

9

"Yeah." The tall young fellow scowled. "Say, Turkey, why'd yuh run off from us? Yuh took that money for yoreself, didn't yuh?"

The man who had called himself Harris Evers turned back to the Rio Kid.

"We're in a bad way for food, Mister. Purty near starvin'. Got women and kids with us, too."

"Where yuh headin'?" asked Pryor.

"Well, back for Missouri, I reckon. Most of 'em are, anyways. We drove to Pike's Peak but when we got there we found it was a hoax. No gold or silver around."

An older man, with a close-clipped pepper-and-salt beard, liquor-bleared eyes, and bent of back from long years of stooping over placer mining, came up and joined Evers. He had a cud of tobacco in one leathery cheek and switched it as he stared steadily at Pryor.

"This here is Old Mac, my pardner," Evers explained.

"Howdy," "Old Mac" cackled.

He was a typical sourdough, the Rio Kid saw, probably an inveterate prospector who all his life had been bitten by the mining bug and had indulged in a feverish search for precious metals. Three more men straggled up but they were of a different type from Old Mac. They looked like greenhorns, out of place in this wilderness.

The Rio Kid hesitated. Like all Western men would have been in the same circumstances, he was firm in the belief that Turkey Craw needed hanging. But these other men looked all right and showed no belligerency toward the Rio Kid because of Turkey Craw. In fact, they seemed to be on Pryor's side, eyeing the sniveling thief with dislike.

"Tickle his ribs and see if he has our cash," suggested Old Mac.

"I—I didn't mean to take it!" sobbed Turkey. "I just happened to—"

Old Mac, assisted by Harris Evers, searched Turkey who was again prostrate on the ground and removed two bags of silver and bills from inside his shirt.

"Yeah, this is it," declared Evers. "He swiped money

10

from several of our folks. But mebbe we shouldn't be too hard on him. It's been a tough pull for him as well as everybody else and our grub's mighty low. Stand up, Turkey."

Turkey Craw managed to stand erect but he was shivering. Had he shown the slightest fight, the Rio Kid might have killed him without compunction, but the man was altogether too abject to waste a bullet on him; sickeningly so. Pryor booted him hard where it would do the most good, lifting him clear of the ground. Turkey Craw yelped and ran away, over the ridge.

The Rio Kid shrugged and turned to Harris Evers and Old Mac, who grinned at Turkey's frightened speed.

"He's been a nuisance all along," remarked Old Mac. "Fool acts like he ain't got good sense sometimes."

"What's yore handle, Mister?" Evers inquired of Pryor.

"Bob Pryor. They call me the Rio Kid. I been huntin' sheep in the peaks."

Old Mac smacked his lips. "I'd sell my soul for a joint of mutton right now," he muttered.

The other men appeared to be hungry, too.

"There's some meat I dropped back a ways," the Rio Kid said, "and plenty more up above."

"We ought to take some to the folks," said Evers.

"Let's have a look," growled Pryor, his curiosity aroused. "Yuh start walkin' back, and I'll overtake yuh."

CHAPTER II

Leadville

☐ The Rio Kid had to return Houston before he could go to the wagon train with his visitors. With the horses belonging to his friends, who were not yet down from their hunt, he left a scribbled note telling where he had gone. Then, riding back on the trail of Evers, Old Mac and the rest, the Rio Kid topped the ridge and looked down on a mountain park in which some canvas-topped wagons were drawn up.

Thirty miles away, the towering façade of Pike's Peak gleamed in the light, with neighboring peaks sticking to the heavens.

The Rio Kid pushed the dun up to the wagons. They were, most of them, worn out, from a long trip across the plains and into the Rockies, and displayed many home-made repairs. Several had painted on their sides the motto,

"PIKE'S PEAK OR BUST!"

Then this had been crudely lined out, and

"BUSTED!"

written underneath.

Around a smoldering campfire were gathered about sixty people, men, and a dozen women, wives and daughters, and some children. They turned their peaked faces toward the Rio Kid. His well-knit, self-assured figure seemed to give them fresh confidence.

The Rio Kid took them in. They were decent-looking Americans, whose dream of quick wealth had been rudely shattered. They had few goods, and little money left, after investing all in equipment for the rush to Pike's Peak.

"Meet the Rio Kid, folks," said Harris Evers, coming over to Pryor. He nodded toward a man at the fire. "This here is Sam Wilton. He's captain of our train."

The heavy-set, good-natured-looking man got up and held out his hand, smiling at Pryor. He had a close-cropped dark beard, thick brows, a good nose and brown hair. He wore old but clean and mended miner's clothing, with blue pants tucked into brogans, a felt hat, and a blue shirt.

"Glad to know yuh, Rio Kid," Wilton said heartily. "Evers has just been sayin' yuh offered us some meat—and I'm shore mighty sorry 'bout Turkey Craw tryin' to steal yore hosses. I should've run him out of the party long ago but he begs so hard I always let him stick."

Turkey Craw was hiding somewhere, but he probably would show up again, like a bad penny.

The Rio Kid shook hands with several of the leading men, nodded to the others.

The Rio Kid's glance, moving about the company, finally came to rest on a slender girl who stood in the shadow of a big wagon. He had an eye for beauty, and the girl, about eighteen or nineteen years old, was pretty in her pink calico dress. Her curly hair was taffy-colored, and her big eyes, long-lashed, had a violet hue. Her well-molded features had a healthy outdoors look.

"My daughter, Dorothy," Sam Wilton said, seeing Pryor's interest.

"How do yuh do," the Rio Kid said to her.

13

She nodded, without speaking, and for a moment held his eyes. Then she looked down.

"My wife's dead," Wilton continued. "Dorothy takes care of me."

Pryor hardly needed to be told that, for her hands showed how hard she worked.

Wilton acted as spokesman for the party, with Harris Evers putting in a word now and then.

We teamed up back in St. Joe," explained Wilton. "All of us strong for goin' to Pike's Peak and makin' our fortune there. It was said all yuh need do was scratch the dirt to turn up gold and silver."

"That's what George Smothers said," amended Harris Evers.

"Smothers?" repeated the Rio Kid.

"Yeah—he's a big dealer in St. Joe and sells supplies and outfits to the wagon trains headin' west. Smothers told us there was a fortune for us here."

"Why, there was a big fake run to Pike's Peak just 'fore the War," exclaimed the Rio Kid.

Wilton shrugged. "Yeah, we heard tell of it. Smothers swore that the fellers who made it missed the real deposits, and shore convinced us. He showed us some gold samples he said come from the Peak. He must've sold forty thousand dollars worth of stuff on this hoax. We didn't find anything worth diggin' up above."

The Rio Kid had run upon victims of a common enough trick, a gold rush started by scheming dealers who stood to profit by the sale of supplies. There had been others of them taken in by the same hoax—too many of them—since that first "Pike's Peak or Bust" rush back in '59.

"Why not try Leadville?" suggested Pryor. "We met an hombre from there last week and he says it's goin' great guns."

Evers slapped his thigh. "That's what I say, Rio Kid. Old Mac and me are headin' there, but there's some who don't believe anything now, not after what we been through. We swung off the regular trail, meanin' to go to Leadville. But all we've done is argue."

"It's a real strike up there," declared the Rio Kid.

"Father," said Dorothy Wilton suddenly, "let's go back home to Pennsylvania."

Wilton smiled at her. "The girl don't fancy minin' life, Rio Kid. Can't say I blame her. Her mother died on a run I made last year to Oregon."

"Well, let's go pack in as much meat as we can and have a feed," Evers suggested. "And after we eat we'll vote once and for all. I'm willin' to travel back to Missouri to help the folks make it, but then Old Mac and me are headin' into the Rockies for Leadville."

The Rio Kid accompanied half a dozen of the younger men, driving a flat wagon, over the rough way to the point where they could reach the mountain sheep that had been shot. They found Bat Masterson and Celestino Mireles making ready to follow their friend, the Rio Kid.

Bat Masterson was young and debonair. He had already made a name for himself among men of highest courage. He was quick of eye and stealthy of foot, an ace shot.

He had a well-shaped head, a cornsilk mustache, and smooth-shaven cheeks. He was a dandy where dress was concerned, and now he wore a red silk bandanna about his neck, and his spurs were gold-inlaid. His gray Stetson was circled by a braided gold and silver band in the shape of a rattlesnake with red glass eyes. He wore a red sash, and buckskins, and carried twin Colts in his cartridge belts. Under his leg, as he sat Houston, was a heavy Sharps .50-caliber buffalo gun. Its name was Marie.

Celestino Mireles hailed the Rio Kid with joy.

"Ah, General! We jus' follow you!"

The Mexican youth, whom Pryor had rescued from Border bandits and who had since clung to him as his trail comrade, was bony and tall. He had a patrician face with a hawk beak, and lively black eyes. He wore the clinging, soft and becoming clothing of his people—velvet pants, short jacket, and a peaked sombrero.

15

The Rio Kid introduced his friends to the miners. He quickly told Bat and Celestino how he had come upon Turkey Craw stealing their horses.

Bat snorted, his gray-blue eyes darkening.

"Yuh should've ventilated the polecat's hide, Rio Kid!"

The Rio Kid shrugged. Turkey Craw had grovelled so that no man would have cared to use an honest Colt on him.

They went on, afoot, leaving their horses and the wagon below, to pick up the sheep the three had killed. Before dark they were back at the wagon train and the hungry people were getting ready for a real meal.

After supper, the vote of which Evers had spoken was taken. Perhaps the strength given by the meat, perhaps the magnetic power of the Rio Kid, turned the scales. The vote was to go on to Leadville and further search for precious metals.

"Will you fellers help us over there?" Sam Wilton eagerly asked the Rio Kid.

The Rio Kid hesitated. Dorothy Wilton was watching him, not speaking, from the shadows outside the circle of dancing firelight.

"All right," agreed the Rio Kid. "I'll tag along. I'd like to see Leadville."

A pretty face and a pair of violet eyes had turned the Rio Kid toward wild adventure high in the rarefied air of the Rockies, where death and menace threatened.

And he was glad that he had so decided. He knew something of Leadville, the wildest, maddest mining town of them all, but not enough to satisfy him. He must see it for himself. And when he finally reached the town the Rio Kid, who had traveled thousands of miles on the Frontier and visited many a boom settlement and mushroom growth, quickly learned that anything he had heard of Leadville was no exaggeration.

For weeks the Rio Kid and Bat Masterson led the prospectors toward their destination, up through the Royal Gorge of the Arkansas River, a narrow gap with breathtaking thousand-foot-high rock sides which provided the

16

only possible route to Leadville for wheeled vehicles. The hunters' accurate rifles kept them in meat.

It was late in June when they arrived at their Golconda. They at once went into camp on a slope a mile from the humming beehive of treasure-hopped humanity.

As soon as the animals had been unhitched and camp made, the men hurried to look over Leadville. Food, equipment, had to be found in one way or another, for they were nearly destitute.

"Some scenery, ain't it, Rio Kid?" exclaimed young Bat Masterson admiringly, as they rode slowly along a rocky road, with Mireles riding behind them.

They were ahead of the men from the wagon train, most of whom were afoot, but Pryor's mind still was on the responsibility he had undertaken to care for the wagon train people.

"It's beautiful country," he declared. "Shore hope the folks hereabouts live up to their country's looks."

Over them loomed a huge mountain, Mt. Massive. Though the little gulch in which Leadville's quaterbillion dollars in lead and silver were being dug was nearly eleven thousand feet in altitude, the peaks rose even higher, their steep sides fringed by growth for a thousand feet more. Above timberline, at eleven thousand, five hundred feet were bare rocks, with patches of snow plainly visible on them.

The wind puffed at the new arrivals from the town.

"Phew!" exclaimed Bat, sniffing.

"Sulphur from the lead smelters, I reckon," the Rio Kid remarked.

They pushed into Leadville, a sprawling settlement of wooden shacks and larger structures.

" 'Harrison Avenue'," read the Rio Kid aloud, on a street sign. "Looks like they shoot wide with their names, Bat."

The "Avenue" was narrow, no more than a rutted mud way. High board sidewalks ran along its length on both sides. State Street was in the same condition, as were the byways and alleys of the town.

Tents, and all sorts of temporary shelters had been thrown up in every available spot, for Leadville had grown too fast in inhabitants to accommodate the eager fortune-seekers who were flocking in by the thousands. Garbage and tin cans lay uncollected in the gutters, with flies by the million swarming over them.

There were men about but it was work time and most citizens were busy digging in the side gulches for themselves or swinging a pick for luckier adventurers whose claims had already panned out.

TABOR'S OPERA HOUSE—TABOR'S HOTEL—TABOR'S GENERAL STORE— TABOR'S BAKERY—TABOR'S FIRE HOUSE.

The Rio Kid saw a number of shining new buildings, most of them marked with the name "Tabor."

"This Tabor hombre must be some punkins, Bat," he observed. "But I'm dry. Let's get a drink."

As the three handsome young riders dismounted, tossing their reins across the hitch-rack in front of

TABOR'S GILTEDGE SALOON

there was a hoarse shout from over the rutted street, a sudden uproar including some gunshots.

Glancing that way, the Rio Kid and his friends saw a small man with a white beard and mustache run with surprising speed from between two buildings. A shot cracked and he immediately ducked behind a thick curb post.

"Help!" he yelled. "Help!"

Half a dozen men in rough clothing—corduroys and felt hats—wearing Colts, and two with other guns in hand and shooting galloped on the venerable victim's trail.

"There he is, boys!" bawled their leader, a powerful,

tow-haired fellow, with a round head and a flat-featured face.

He fired again and cut a chunk of wood from the post sheltering the unarmed quarry.

"Say, Bat, he's sorta advanced in years for that sorta game," growled the Rio Kid. "I'm goin' to horn in."

"Help!" shouted the victim again.

The Rio Kid galloped across the rutted street, with Bat and Celestino at his spurs. The white-bearded man turned bright eyes on him as Pryor asked:

"What's wrong, Grandpa?"

"They're lot-jumpers!" yelped the old fellow. "I—I own a big lot next street. They're buildin' on it and—and threaten to kill me if—I don't give it up! That's Bull Olsen, and he—"

"Stand away, there," the big man in the lead snarled, pausing a few paces from the Rio Kid, who now stood in front of the white-beard.

However, the aspect of the three armed Frontiersmen had cooled the ardor of some of the gunmen. Deliberately the Rio Kid pushed to the fore, standing with his hands hanging easy by his holstered Colts.

"What's the idee of gunnin' an unarmed citizen?" he demanded.

"Keep outa this!" the big leader snapped. "Or yuh'll be pushin' up grassroots tonight, hombre!"

CHAPTER III

Lawless Town

☐ Coolly the Rio Kid appraised the man who had threatened him. The fellow had a huge body, arms as big as most men's legs, a flat, rather vacuous face, baby-blue eyes and tow hair under a felt hat. A blue shirt covered his great bearlike torso, a shirt opened to show the albino hair on his chest. His corduroys were held up by red suspenders, but he wore a wide belt to carry guns and the bullets for them, and tremendous hobnailed boots.

"He's Bull Olsen," the oldster whom the Rio Kid was protecting said, pointing. "He's a bad hombre. Look out he don't shoot yuh while yore back's turned, Mister. The whole passel of 'em ought to be in Boot Hill!"

The men with "Bull" Olsen were of the same stamp as he, hard of eye, bearded, dirty, in mixed clothing of range and mine, and all were armed. They waited for Olsen's decision.

"Who are you, Grandpa?" the Rio Kid inquired of the oldster.

"Well, they call me Nevada Charlie," replied the white-beard. "I own a lot over there on State Street, like I said, and it's worth plenty. I was out of town for a few days and when I come back this mornin' durned if I didn't see Olsen and a bunch of his friends startin' to put up a saloon on my land! I tried to stop 'em and they would've kilt me only I ducked and run."

"He's lyin'!" Olsen growled quickly. "The old goat's loco. He sold me that lot the other night when he was full of red-eye. . . . Get outa my way!"

As again he challenged the Rio Kid, Olsen lunged forward, reaching for "Nevada Charlie." The Rio Kid, lithe and trained, though outweighed by a hundred pounds, seized Olsen's wrist, fell aside, and by Olsen's own strength mainly, sent the big Swede crashing on his belly and face in the gutter.

It was neatly done, a good wrestler's trick. The breath was jolted from Olsen, but he had a bull's power and came up on his knees, roaring with outraged pain. The Rio Kid was laughing at him, and the infuriated man, gun still clasped in his great paw, swung and threw his Colt to firing level.

The Rio Kid made his own draw then. It was so fast the eye could not follow the blurred hand. The Army Colt leaped to his trained grip, the hammer spur back under thumb rising, and then the Rio Kid's weapon snarled.

Olsen's lead kicked up dirt between Pryor's spread boots, missing entirely. Bull's mouth opened, the light stubble sticking out around his dirt-smeared cheeks. The pistol no longer was in his grip and he stared dumbly at his slashed, bleeding hand, numbed from the wound dealt him by the Rio Kid.

At that every man present dug for his shooting-irons.

Bat Masterson and Celestino Mireles fired a breath later. Several Colts barked together, the powder-smoke curling into the wind. The Rio Kid let go once more, and three of the gunsters facing them went out of action, one falling and rolling over on his face. The others were winged through the shoulder. The survivors turned and ran between the houses, yelling shrilly.

"Some shootin'!" Nevada Charlie yelped. "Who are yuh, hombre—Buffalo Bill or Hickok?"

"Neither." Pryor grinned at the admiring old man. "This here is Bat Masterson and I'm the Rio Kid."

"Well, doggone! That explains it." Nevada Charlie was highly pleased. "I mighta knowed yuh was quality. I've heard of yuh both. And thanks a million for savin' my hide from the lowest passel of polecats in Colorado—in fact, I'd say west of Missouri." He added that judiciously, glaring at Bull Olsen.

Olsen crouched where he was, holding his smashed right hand, the nerves of which were beginning to telegraph the pain. His baby-blue eyes popped out with fear. He expected death.

"Get!" snarled the Rio Kid, slapping the big man's face so hard it sounded like a pistol shot.

Olsen got up, turned and started away. The Rio Kid hurried him with a kick in the right place. The Swede had no more fight in him.

"C'mon, Grandpa, and we'll get yore lot back for yuh," Pryor offered. "Might as well make it whole hog or none, eh, Bat?"

Led by Nevada Charlie, they hustled over toward State Street. The shooting had attracted some attention, and several men were hurrying toward the spot where the Rio Kid and Bat had tangled with Olsen.

"There they are, and on their hosses!" cried Nevada Charlie, pointing as they came out among the piles of refuse and garbage thrown into the back alleys, and could see through to State.

A dozen more men, all armed, were lined up on a corner lot. With them, having brought the warning that Olsen was down, were two who had escaped the Rio Kid, Masterson and Mireles.

"Stand back, Grandpa!" ordered the Rio Kid. "We'll handle this."

Masterson, Mireles and Pryor walked straight toward the line of enemies across State Street, hands swinging loose at their hips.

It was four to one, but the Rio Kid and his partners enjoyed odds. Separated by several feet, abreast, the three defenders marched steadily onward. Half-way across the road, where some lumber and stone had been dumped for building, the chief of the gang on the lot hailed them.

"Stop where yuh are or we'll fire!"

They were hard-looking fellows, of the stamp of Bull Olsen and his mates with whom the trio had already tangled.

The Rio Kid kept walking, and a panicky gunman pulled the trigger of his Colt. The slug sailed wide over Pryor's head and an instant later the fellow doubled up, screaming, struck by the Rio Kid's lead.

The ball opened fast. Olsen's men fired a volley, and Bat Masterson swore, feeling the nip of a bullet in the flesh of his left arm. It did not disturb Bat's aim, however, and he and the two men siding him began shooting steadily, taking that bit of time vital to accurate fire.

Every shot they let go counted, and by the time they reached the curb, the lot-jumpers, half of them cut up, broke and ran away, leaving two unmoving on the ground.

Victorious, with the jubilant, cackling Nevada Charlie dashing up to join them, the Rio Kid and his mates held the field.

However, the heavy gunfire had roused others in Leadville who were not too preoccupied with their personal affairs, and citizens were coming from every direction toward the scene. Among the first to gallop up was a stocky, powerful man with a square, rugged face, blue eyes, and dark hair showing beneath his felt hat. He wore double belts of cartridges and a city marshal's star was pinned to his vest.

He took one look at the wounded and dead.

"What in thunder's goin' on here—a slaughter?" he bellowed. "What yuh doin' with them guns?"

He glared belligerently at the Rio Kid and Bat Masterson.

The Rio Kid coolly surveyed the Law.

"It's all right, Marshal," he drawled, not liking the marshal's bellicose manner much, but unwilling to buck an officer. "We were fired on and defended ourselves."

"That's what you say," snarled the lawman, bristling up to the Rio Kid and sticking out his prognathous jaw. "You cheap tinhorn gunnies can't shoot up my town and get away with it! Why, I'll—"

There would have been a fight but Nevada Charlie seized the marshal's arm and pulled him around, shrieking:

"Marty—Marty, cut it out! These young fellers saved my life! Bull Olsen and his crowd tried to jump my lot just now."

The marshal was scowling and he was a tough man, ready to fight anybody. However, Nevada Charlie made him hesitate.

"This is Marty Duggan, best danged lawman in the country," Nevada Charlie went on quickly, with a wink at the Rio Kid. "Shake hands, Marty, with Bat Masterson, the Rio Kid, and their Mex pard, name of Mireles."

Duggan was somewhat mollified. "Oh, that's who yuh be," he growled. "Yeah, this here is Charlie's lot, all right. They was jumpin' it, huh? By glory, I'll fix the dirty thieves."

He began kickin' a wounded lot-jumper nearby, venting his temper on the Olsen gunny.

The Rio Kid shrugged, turned away.

"Say, Bat, let's have that drink we started after when we was interrupted."

The three friends hurried off, but were overtaken by Nevada Charlie as they crossed Harrison Avenue.

"Oh no yuh don't, gents!" cried the old fellow. "Yuh can't pay for drinks in this town, Rio Kid! They're on me."

Entering the Giltedge Saloon, they lined up at the ornate bar. Miners, gamblers, speculators, boomers, thieves, and many other brands of humanity were in the large place, and talk hummed loud. Nevada Charlie was grinning widely with his toothless jaws as he proudly introduced the Rio Kid and his companions to acquaintances. He was an old-timer around Leadville and known to all.

He carried a fat purse and would not allow the three to pay for food or liquor.

"Yuh saved my hide, gents, to say nothin' of that lot!" he kept insisting. "Drink up."

Evening was at hand. The shadows grew deeper as the Rio Kid and his friends enjoyed themselves in the Giltedge. As Darkness fell over the shadowed gulch in which Leadville stood, the day shift in the lead carbonate and silver mines quit, and came roaring into town for food, drink and wassail. The streets grew crowded with jostling, rough-tongued mining men. Saloons filled to overflowing, and music, yelps, and gunshots rang out.

Oil lamps were lighted, and in their softening rays Leadville did not look quite so tawdry and dirty as in the bright glare of the day.

"What say we take a walk around?" suggested the Rio Kid. "Maybe we better see what our friends are up to."

But as they prepared to go outside, filled with food and drink by the grateful Nevada Charlie, there was an uproar at the front batinds.

"Wait, boys, here comes the mayor!" Charlie cried.

They paused in shouldering through the crowded bar, staring at the door. A heavy-bodied man of middle age, with a fat stomach, short legs, and a round, genial face lighted by a wide smile, slowly entered the Giltedge. Baldness had crept in over his temples and gray showed in his once dark hair.

The outstanding characteristic of his facial make-up, however, was his mustache. It was simply tremendous, thick and black, glossy, and as big as a floor mop. It stretched for inches in its glorious width and was waxed and turned up until it practically touched the big man's eyes.

His clothing was extremely elegant. Tight-fitting doeskin pants came to the tops of his soft calfskin boots of high grade. He wore a white ruffled shirt and stock, a black frock coat with a velvet vest, and a pure gold, heavy watch-chain studded with real diamonds. A diamond solitarie as big as a hazel nut sparkled in his tie, and

25

he affected more of the precious stones in rings on his thick, stubby hands.

Despite the wealth of his garb, and his evident importance, he had an oafish look. His blue eyes were prominent, like a frog's, popping out as he glanced about.

His route to the bar was marked by numerous back-slappings, both on the mayor's part and on the part of others who slapped his broad back.

"That's the mayor, huh?" grunted Bat Masterson, a faint smile touching his lips at sight of the Number One celebrity of Leadville.

"That's shore him." Nevada Charlie nodded. "Horace Austin Warner Tabor, to tell it all. The hombre who really discovered California Gulch—that's Leadville. Like to shake hands with him? He's an old friend of mine. I used to know him when he didn't have a dollar but what his wife Augusta earned bakin' bread and cakes for the prospectors. The Tabors kept a little store in the Gulch.

"One day a couple of no-goods begged a grub-stake from Tabor, and in his big-hearted way he had also given them a bottle of whiskey. They didn't get far, on account of the likker and bein' full, they just started diggin' near at hand where they happened to be. Struck the Little Pittsburgh Mine. Twenty thousand a week in ore, and them boys cut in 'good old Tabor' as they called him, on account of that whiskey he gave 'em for a third share!"

"That's luck for yuh," the Rio Kid observed. "He shore expanded."

That was the word for Mayor Tabor, expansive. Everybody knew him, and practically everybody liked him. Tabor's "luck" had become famous. Everything he touched brought him wealth, and he was already in possession of a large fortune. His heart was as big as his purse and he never refused to help those less fortunate than himself.

Tabor, reaching the bar, was instantly surrounded by everybody in the saloon who was not pinned down.

"Drink up, boys, on the house!" Tabor bellowed happily.

Nevada Charlie sought to circle around the excited crowd, hunting a way through to Tabor so as to introduce his new friends, but there was not a gap in the ranks.

"Dog it," Charlie growled, "they're like a bunch of ants round a honeypot. They're—"

He broke off. The saloon was in uproar, with shouted jests and greetings, the clink of bottles. Nevada Charlie looked around, toward an open window which gave out on a side alleyway.

"Hey!" he bawled. "Somebody just took a shot at me!"

Charlie had slapped a hand to his ear. As he took it down and stared at it, the Rio Kid saw the red blood from the gash in the oldster's ear. A slug had come within half an inch of finishing Charlie's career.

"Who busted that mirror!" an angry bartender roared, pointing at a crack in the glass. The bullet, nicking Nevada Charlie's ear, had gone over the heads of those at the bar and into the mirror.

The talk ceased for a moment. Tabor and his friends looked around to see what was happening.

"They're tryin' to kill me!" Charlie yelled.

Tabor put out his hands as though swimming, and came through the crowd toward the angry old fellow.

"What's up, Charlie?" the mayor demanded.

"Hey, Horace—listen!" the old fellow said swiftly. "Bull Olsen and his gang tried to jump my lot this afternoon, and the only reason I'm standin' here is these gents. Meet the Rio Kid and Bat Masterson. The Mex is named Celestino—er—Mireles."

"Gentlemen, it's a pleasure!" Tabor said in his chronically loud voice. He slapped Bat, the Rio Kid, and the Mexican on the back with hearty geniality, and shook hands. "Drink up—on me, please."

"Glad to know yuh, Mayor." The Rio Kid smiled. It was impossible not to like such a genial soul.

"Yuh say someone fired on yuh?" asked Tabor, his eyes boring at Nevada Charlie.

"Yeah. From that winder. I was movin' or I'd be dead, Horace. It was Olsen or one of his men."

"Yuh see him?"

"Nope. But I'm shore of it."

Tabor's moon face reddened. "They are gettin' bolder and bolder, Charlie. It ain't only Olsen either. He's got somebody behind him and they're makin' a bid to take Leadville away from us. They ain't what yuh'd call decent folks, they ain't. Oh, I've had plenty of warnin's—friends whisper things in my ear. Unless it's checked, a lot of plumb innocent folks are goin' to be hurt and crime'll own this here town."

With this prophetic utterance, Tabor turned his bulging gaze on the Rio Kid and Bat Masterson.

"Brave men," he continued quietly, "don't need to be paid for doin' what has to be done, although me, I would not let one who done his duty go unrewarded. Long as I'm in Leadville I'll stand for decency and order and the chance the poor should have."

"That's the truth!" chorused Nevada Charlie. "Yuh've never turned down a man who needed help, Tabor. And that cussed Olsen'll kill me sooner or later. Who yuh reckon is behind him and his gang, Horace?"

Tabor shook his round head. "It's shapin' up, shapin' up, Charlie. Me'n you are old friends, ain't we? We savvy what Leadville is. There ain't any real law save what the *decent* men here stand for." Again his eyes, which shone with kindness, fixed the Rio Kid. "Marty Duggan's a good man. He's liable to go off half-cocked sometimes, and he's quick of temper, and ain't as far-sighted as he might be, though he does his best. But order can't be kept by a lone marshal."

Tabor was talking directly at Bob Pryor, the Rio Kid. The magnetic power of the Rio Kid had impressed Tabor, who was a shrewd judge of human character. He had set forth the case properly, making financial considerations secondary. It would have been an insult to offer cash for such a job as that at which he hinted to the Rio Kid and Bat Masterson, money for itself alone.

Instead, Tabor appealed to their sense of right, violated by Olsen's crude violence. He felt sure that such a plea would sway these men.

CHAPTER IV

Claims

☐ Mayor Tabor was a good psychologist. He had said the thing that alone would appeal to the Rio Kid. For Pryor already was angered at the skulking attempt to drygulch Nevada Charlie.

Leadville knew that Pryor had taken the oldster under his wing, and again Bull had tried to kill Charlie, likely in reprisal this time for what the Rio Kid had done to the big Swede. Throughout the West that was a direct challenge, and the Rio Kid was not the man to back down from such.

Silence had fallen about Tabor as he faced the Rio Kid, his plea completed. As Nevada Charlie had declared, the mayor was a square-shooter, a benefactor of the unfortunate, his purse ever ready to help those in need. Despite his bizarre appearance, Horace Tabor was as kind a man as the Frontier had ever produced. Riduclous in many ways, to the thinking of some, yet he was courageous and would never say die.

"Where does this Olsen polecat usually hang out?" drawled the Rio Kid, when an answer seemed necessary.

Tabor had put it squarely up to the Rio Kid and Bat Masterson. He had done so in public and there was only one answer for a man of such strength of body and moral courage as those two possessed.

"Usually Bull hangs out over at Dinty's, a dive on State Street," answered Charlie. "Next block, that is."

"What say, Bat?" asked Pryor.

Masterson grinned, nodded.

"Awful passel of toughs in Dinty's," warned Nevada Charlie.

"That ain't the way to discourage the Rio Kid, bucko," Bat Masterson smiled.

Horace Tabor reached in his jacket pocket, and brought forth two small silver badges. One of them he pinned on the Rio Kid's vest, the other on Bat Masterson's. Etched on each badge was, "*Special Deputy*." It was a challenge from the decent element in Leadville, just as Olsen had challenged from the evil side.

The Rio Kid swung on his high-heeled riding boots and, followed by his friends, left the saloon.

"Show me Dinty's, Charlie," he ordered quietly, when they were outside.

He had his name to make in Leadville as he had made it elsewhere, and his pride as a fighting man to uphold. By maintaining such power, the Rio Kid was able to help others, such as the needy folks he had guided through the Rockies.

The quartet hurried up Harrison Avenue, and swung the corner under a street lamp, walking in the center of the high board sidewalk.

Someone hailed them, and Pryor paused, as Harris Evers and Old Mac ran to them.

"Rio Kid—Bat!" cried Evers. "Where yuh been? We was worried 'bout yuh. Heard there was a ruckus and that yuh was in it. We been huntin' yuh all evenin'. Most of the rest of the folks went back to camp."

"Been busy with this gent," drawled the Rio Kid. "Meet Nevada Charlie. Evers, Old Mac. They're with that Pike's Peak bunch we told yuh about, Charlie. We'll be back to camp 'fore long, Evers. Got some business to tend to on State Street."

31

"Let us go along," begged Evers.

The Rio Kid shrugged. "It may be dangerous, boys. We're goin' into a skunk's den."

"Count me in," Evers said at once, and Old Mac grunted.

They moved on. State Street was the rough thoroughfare of the town and was crammed with disreputable dives of every description. Miners were whooping it up in the joints.

Dinty's was a sprawling place of unpainted mountain logs, glowing with a smoky, purple light. As the new arrivals paused just inside the batwings, the Rio Kid took in the sawdust-covered floor, the fly-covered bar, and the dirty aprons of the barkeepers. Shady, hard-faced characters were about, some drinking, some playing cards at tables. A tinny piano was being banged in a corner, and girls in gaudy dresses circulated among the rioting miners who were being trimmed.

"Olsen's usually in the big back parlor," Nevada Charlie told the Rio Kid. "Watch it, now, if yuh go there. It's right through that door, to yore left hand."

The Rio Kid strolled through the saloon, his friends at his heels. Passing through a wide doorway, he glanced to his left and could see into a rear room in which were chairs and a couple of round tables, a hanging lamp with tobacco smoke clinging to its heat, and spittoons. Here a dozen men were seated, drinking and talking. Among them was Bull Olsen, a rough bandage tied about his right hand that had been wounded when the Rio Kid had shot a pistol from his fingers that afternoon.

When Olsen saw the Rio Kid slouched in the entry, a scared look came into his baby-blue eyes. His chin dropped and he choked out a curse.

A big man seated at Olsen's right had thick black hair, and a crisp, close-clipped beard that ornamented his strong jaw. His skin was swarthy, he had keen black eyes, a hawk nose, and straight lips. He wore a dark suit, and his narrow-brimmed hat lay on the table.

A wiry little fellow in a brown suit, with a red-skinned

32

face shaven smooth, and nervous gray eyes, sat at the other side of the bearded man. He glanced quickly toward the door as he read Olsen's alarm, and nudged the black-beard, saying something in an undertone.

The important-looking man seated beside Olsen looked toward the Rio Kid, who stepped into the room.

"What do you want?" the man with the black beard demanded. "This is a private room, sir."

"What I got to say is private—with Bull Olsen," the Rio Kid answered carelessly. "No one'll get hurt if he keeps his hands in sight, savvy? I want a word with Olsen."

The rest of the men in the room stiffened. They were some of the lot-jumpers, tough fellows, who had been with Olsen that afternoon.

Bat Masterson came in and took the left side of the doorway. Nevada Charlie was behind Pryor, as were Evers, Old Mac, and Celestino Mireles.

"I come to tell yuh, Olsen," the Rio Kid said evenly, "that I wasn't foolin' this afternoon. If anything happens to Nevada Charlie in Leadville, I hold you responsible. Yuh savvy what that means?"

"I dunno what yuh're talkin' about," growled Bull.

"Yore drygulcher missed at the Giltedge. For yore own health, make shore no more shots are fired at Charlie. He's a pard of mine—a pard of the Rio Kid."

"That goes for me, too, Olsen," Bat Masterson drawled.

Olsen looked worried. He glanced quickly at the man with the black beard.

There was a sudden curse and a bustle behind the Rio Kid. It was Harris Evers, pushing to the fore. Old Mac was at his heels, and Evers, ignoring everybody else, jumped toward the man with the dark beard who was sitting with Bull Olsen.

"Smothers! George Smothers! How in tarnation do you come to be in Leadville?"

Smothers frowned. He stared into young Evers' serious eyes. It was plain he didn't recognize the prospector.

33

"I don't recollect havin' the pleasure, sir," he said in his gruff voice, which had a cold ring to it.

"Don't yuh?" Evers said quietly, standing before Smothers as the man swung around in his seat. "Mebbe there was so many folks yuh fooled that yuh couldn't recall every face. It was back in St. Joe, and yuh told of how much gold there was for us all at Pike's Peak. There was thousands took in by that hoax, Smothers. My friends put all their money in equipment yuh sold at a fat profit. Six folks died durin' the journey, from bein' hungry and cold and wet. One was a kid."

Intrigued, the Rio Kid watched, listening to Evers' cool even voice as he accused Smothers.

"Now I wonder!" Pryor mused. "Is this Smothers snake the hombre buckin' Tabor in town?"

George Smothers did not fancy the conversation. A red glow shone in the depths of his snapping eyes, which narrowed and blinked rapidly as rage burned his brain. The Rio Kid felt intuitively that Smothers was the most dangerous man among the group around the table, much more virulent and clever than the Swede of the pale blue eyes or the nervous little fellow by his side.

"What's all this to me?" snapped Smothers. "I believed the yarns about the Peak, that's all. Of course I made a profit on my sales. That's legal, ain't it?"

"Oh, yeah, it was all legal, I reckon." Evers nodded quietly. His speech was so mild that what he did was doubly startling. His powerful hand, toughened by shovel and pick, flashed out and slapped Smothers in the face. It sounded like a pistol shot, and Evers hit so hard that Smothers was knocked over backward in his chair, and rolled in the dirty sawdust.

Bat Masterson's pistol suddenly exploded—one of Olsen's gunmen on the far side of the room had stealthily drawn a revolver, as eyes turned to the sprawling, cursing Smothers. Bat's bullet cut a chunk from the killer's shoulder and the man began to yip in agony.

The Rio Kid, leaping in, slashed at Bull Olsen with the

barrel of his Colt, and Olsen joined Smothers on the floor.

Masterson, the Rio Kid, and Mireles, guns ready in hand, stood with spread feet, ready for a fight if the gunnies wanted it.

But none of the Rio Kid's opponents seemed willing to draw lead from such fighting men's guns as covered them. Smothers, Olsen, and the rest of the lot-jumpers froze in position under the steady Colts.

The Rio Kid, seeing them cowed, spoke slowly.

"Remember, gents. I hold yuh responsible for the lives of my friends, savvy? If so much as a hair of their heads is touched, so help me I'll clean out yore whole nest of rats!"

"I'll remember, Rio Kid," George Smothers said, his teeth gritted.

His eyes were blinking rapidly, burning with hatred. But he made no overt move, remaining on one knee, a hand steadying him as he met the Rio Kid's gaze full.

Nevada Charlie's high-itched cackle rang out.

"They're yeller, the whole passel of 'em!" he crowed. "Bull, yuh've met yore match. I reckon I can walk out at night now without expectin' a bullet in the back. I'll make Leadville too hot to hold yuh, 'cause the mayor's a friend of mine. Yore thievin' schemes will be nipped in the bud if I have anything to say."

"Let's go, boys," ordered the Rio Kid.

He waved his comrades from the room, being the last to leave—walking backward, and with his gun ready in case someone decided to try a quick one as they left.

However, their retreat was in good order and nobody moved to stop them.

"Let's go back to the Giltedge and celebrate, Rio Kid!" Nevada Charlie grinned, slapping Pryor on the back. "Yuh're a man after my own heart. Anything I got belongs to yuh."

Charlie was walking beside the Rio Kid, his back toward Harrison Avenue.

"Looka here, Rio Kid," he went on eagerly. "I got a

35

silver claim up the Gulch, and from now on it's yores. I'll sign it over to yuh first thing in the mornin'."

Pryor laughed. "No need to do that, Charlie. Keep yore claim. Bat and me and Celestino are no diggers. And yuh don't have to pay me for the sport we just had. If yuh want to, yuh can give them folks who come here with me yore advice, mebbe a grubstake."

"I didn't think yuh'd take it," Nevada Charlie said regretfully. "As for yore pards, Rio Kid, don't worry. I won't forgit 'em and neither'll Tabor."

CHAPTER V

A Threat

☐ Back in Dinty's, the low dive on State Street where Olsen and Smothers had been so rudely handled by the Rio Kid and his party, fresh drinks were ordered and the lot jumpers resumed their seats at the round table. The wounded man had been sent to the doctor's to have his injury dressed.

Murderous rage against the Rio Kid and all those who had bearded them in their den burned in the hearts of the rough lot.

"Squirrel" Hart, the wiry little fellow who was George Smothers' constant companion and idea man, sat hunched over his glass. Smothers had brushed the worst of the sawdust from his clothing, and was choking on his humiliation. Bull Olsen was mouthing loud, cursing threats.

"I'll kill every one of them sons!" Olsen declared, now that the danger was past.

"Dry up, Bull," Smothers ordered testily. "You had your chance and you acted like a scared hound."

"Well, I was under the gun, wasn't I?" Bull said aggrievedly.

"Better not touch 'em, not for a while, anyways, Boss," Squirrel Hart suggested. "We ain't consolidated yet in

Leadville. We need more men so's we can handle anything. This Rio Kid and Nevada Charlie will prove prime nuisances, I'm afeared. Charlie has Tabor's ear and they'll spread the word we're crooked. That will make it hard for us to pull off any of the deals we figgered on. We're licked 'fore we start."

"I won't quit now," growled Smothers, his fingers white as he gripped his glass of whiskey. "I'll kill the Rio Kid and I'll kill Evers, too, for darin' to lay hands on me!"

"That's the way to talk!" crowed Bull Olsen.

"Only the boss means it, Bull," Squirrel Hart told him silkily. "It ain't just talk with him."

"You're right, though, Squirrel," Smothers went on more calmly. "I won't strike until I'm ready. Bull, remember that. You make yourself scarce for a few days, till this blows over. Collect as many fighters as possible, and I'll decide what to do next. Too bad that Evers and Wilton bunch had to show up here. It interferes with my plans."

There were untold millions of dollars in Leadville, millions coveted by George Smothers, whose evil brain was lit with its metallic lure. His sharp practices as a merchant back in other states had netted him many thousands of dollars, but the elusive big killing he craved had never come.

His reputation had grown shady in St. Joe. The propaganda which he had put out concerning Pike's Peak had boomeranged on him, and he had found his business falling off after the hoax was exposed.

Then had come the news of the real strike in Leadville, and Smothers, selling out, had hurried to Colorado to get in on the fortunes being picked up by speculators.

Yet only a handful among the thousands who came made any real money. Most of them hit poor claims, or fell by the wayside. It was not a simple matter to win.

Shunning any such physical labor as hunting for a vein of metal in the mountains entailed, Smothers was after big, but easy money. He wanted wealth, metal wealth, gold and silver and lead, that would make him a real power. Not thousands, but millions. He wanted to be a mining king, such as Tabor had become.

Back in his youth Smothers had been poor, a product of city slums. Running away from home after a thieving interlude, he had found work with a St. Joe merchant, and had wormed his way into the childless old man's confidence. Impressed by Smothers' quick mind and apparent affection for him, the merchant had made Smothers his heir.

Soon after he signed his will he died—Smothers had seen to that. There were slow poisons that took several weeks to finish off a victim, and Smothers had made canny use of them and had not been suspected. For of course a man of the merchant's age could die without rousing suspicion.

However, retail thievery had not satisfied George Smothers, and he was now blossoming out, at the beginning of a career of high crime.

Not only had he marked the Rio Kid, Nevada Charlie, and Harris Evers for death, but all who dared block him, large or small. Nothing like compassion had ever touched Smothers' heart.

"I am going to pull Tabor down," declared Smothers. "Eventually I'll own Leadville. Nothing will stop me. He's already uneasy, is Tabor. He senses what is buildin' up. But he can't win, even if he calls in a hundred Rio Kids and Bat Mastersons and fighting Mexicans. Why? Because Tabor is soft at heart. He's had a fool's luck, that's all, and fools can't keep what they grab. The Rio Kid, Evers, the wagon train folks and any others of their friends must die. They're in the way. I can't have that passel of donkeys brayin' against me in Colorado."

Squirrel Hart nodded vigorously.

"Yuh got to keep a clean front, Chief, that's shore."

Like most criminals, these scheming men hated unfavorable limelight. Smothers must maintain the aspect of decency, to fool the general public.

"Yuh know we worked it all out, Boss," Hart went on,

39

"and picked Nevada Charlie as the only big mine owner we could take quick. Tabor and the others have got heirs and pardners, and all kinds of tie-ups. But Nevada Charlie's a lone wolf and ain't got no family. He's Tabor's friend, but they don't own together.

"With Charlie's big Maiden's Prayer Mine in the main Gulch we'd have plenty to start after Tabor and the whole tarnation shebang. That Potato Hole Mine is another of Nevada Charlie's, but they say the cream's skimmed off it. Too bad Bull missed the old goat. It would have give us a real start. With Nevada Charlie dead and our noses clean we could make a fortune."

"We'll get rid of Charlie soon—and the rest," promised Smothers. . . .

Supremely unconcerned about what might be plotted against them—though they knew that that was likely a certainty—the Rio Kid and his friends finally rolled up in their blankets and slept the sleep of the just.

Bat Masterson woke the Rio Kid before dawn, touching his blanketed shoulder.

"Hey, Bob," Masterson said, keeping his voice low so as not to disturb the camp of sleeping prospectors, "I'm leavin'. How about comin' along?"

"What's up?" demanded the Rio Kid, rubbing the sleep from his eyes.

"I woke up an hour or so ago and, bein' restless, I rode into town. Couple of guards for a bullion train done got full of red-eye and disabled last night and we can have their jobs. It pays high, and as for me my funds are low. And I ain't aimin' to dig in the dirt in mines for other hombres."

The Rio Kid thought it over.

"I could use some cash myself, Bat," he confessed. "But I don't want to leave these folks. They need help."

"On the way back, freight pays eighteen dollars a ton, so yuh make both in and out. We'll be back in Leadville inside of a week rollin' in wealth. Yuh can call yore own turn then and I'm with yuh."

"We better go, then. Wait till I speak to Wilton and Evers. They ought to be able to hold out till we return, and as yuh say, we'll be in a better way to boost 'em along after we're paid."

He wanted to help the people he had led to Leadville, but it would take them a few days to shake down and rest up after their ordeal. He had generously bought provisions from his own pocket, and he wanted more cash to use. Masterson's suggestion was a good one.

An hour later, as the dawn came up, the Rio Kid, Bat Masterson and Celestino Mireles rode out of Leadville, headed for the Denver Mint, guarding the wagonloads of heavy silver and lead pigs.

Harris Evers and all the prospectors in the camp were sorry to see the departure of their friends, the Rio Kid, and his hard-bitten partners, but made the best of it.

"We own 'em a lot, for fetchin' us through and advisin' us," declared Evers to Sam Wilton.

The heavy-set, good-humored Wilton nodded, his face sober.

"Yuh reckon they'll come back?" he asked.

Evers shrugged. "Dunno. Said they would, but hombres like them has the itchin' foot—and me, too, Sam. I like to be movin'. Figger Old Mac and me'll take our tools and meander through the mountains hereabouts, to see what we can find."

"Why not stick together, round Leadville?" suggested Wilton. "They say the only real good claims are in the Gulch here."

"'They,'" repeated Evers, with a smile. "'They're' always sayin' somethin', Sam."

At a soft step from the rear of the wagon close to which Wilton and Evers stood conversing that morning, not long after the Rio Kid had left Leadville, Evers glanced around. It was Dorothy, Wilton's daughter.

She seldom had much to say. She was obedient and almost meek with her father, loving him dearly and caring for him as best she could. Evers had come to admire her deeply. She was beautiful, with her wavy light hair and violet eyes, but she also had a depth of character unusual in a girl so young.

Wilton swung away. He had many duties to perform. The new arrivals in Leadville, in their wagon camp, were finishing up breakfast as the sun turned to a golden hue in the rare sky, and he had to be sure they were all right.

"Old Mac's lying dead to the world under the wagon," Dorothy said in a low voice to Evers as her father disappeared.

Evers laughed. "Yeah, when Old Mac gets near a town he'll drink every saloon dry."

"It's sad," Dorothy said. "I don't think it's funny."

Evers looked down into her serious, lovely face. A sudden emotion swept over him. He realized how deeply he was in love with Dorothy Wilton. He caught her hand, and tried to draw her to him, to kiss her. They were on the far side of the wagon and nobody was looking their way. But she turned her lips away.

"Please don't, Harris," she murmured.

"I love yuh, Dorothy," he said eagerly. "I wish yuh'd marry me. Will yuh? When I make my strike I'll cover yuh with diamonds, that's the truth." His fine young eyes burned with what he felt for her.

She looked down, and shook her head. "No, Harris."

"I'd do anything for yuh," he muttered pleadingly.

"Would you really?" she asked, looking up quickly.

"Yes."

"Will you quit prospecting and mining, and settle down?"

"Yuh mean—yuh'd marry me if I did?"

"I might. If you really settled."

Evers perked up. "Yuh mean that? Then yuh must like me, anyhow."

"I love you, Harris," she murmured, her cheeks reddening with soft color.

She let him kiss her now. "When we're rich," Evers cried with the blind optimism of his youthful strength,

"I'll build yuh a mansion, Dorothy! Yuh'll have a carriage and the best that money buys."

"I don't care, as long as I have you," she told him. "You'll quit mining now, won't you?"

Evers bit his lip. It was a hard promise for him to have to make. The prospecting bug had entered his blood and given him a fever it was difficult to cure. The girl watched him, with worry lines corrugating her young brows.

"Let me go out on one more trip with Mac," begged Evers. "We'll strike it this time—I feel it in my bones. Why, one lucky dig with a pick, Dorothy, and we wouldn't have to worry any more."

Her red lips trembled and she turned aside to hide the disappointment in her eyes.

"You don't understand, Harris," she half-whispered. "I can't stand this wandering, gambling life. Father is good to me, and I love him better—well, better than most anything. But I saw my mother fade and die because of his mad hunt for gold and silver. She always wanted a home, a place to rest and be happy, but Father never settled. And Old Mac, look at him! That's the way most of you end up."

She pulled her hand away from Evers, turning.

"I'm afraid you're the same, Harris. If you can show me you're not—"

"Dorothy! Dorothy! C'mere. Where's my short-handled pick?"

That was Sam Wilton, shouting for her.

She hurried away, leaving Evers by the wagon. He was troubled, torn between his love for the girl, and his calling. He did not realize it then, but he was up against a not unusual situation, the woman he wanted to marry desiring steadiness and a settled home, while the male craved excitement, an all-or-nothing gamble for wealth.

The people of the wagon train had come fifteen hundred miles together, sharing what they had. There had been petty squabbles, human nature being what it was, but all in all they had got along well. Only a few had decided to leave the camp. The rest had voted to stay together as long as they could, and Sam Wilton was still their captain.

Turkey Craw, the thief whom the Rio Kid had chastised, had followed them through to Leadville. He had been humble, and had worked as ordered. On probation, Turkey Craw had avoided any further trouble.

But the first night they had camped close enough to the roaring mining town, Turkey Craw had silently slipped away. Evers had seen him on State Street, hanging around the low dives in that district. It was no loss. In fact, everybody had breathed easier to see Turkey Craw leave.

CHAPTER VI

A Lucky Start

☐ High hopes burned anew in the hearts of every man belonging to the wagon train. The Smythe brothers, big, dark-haired men from Ohio who had their own wagon, with their wives and children along, were about to pull out and head into the surrounding canyons, to start the hunt for silver veins. Johnny Burnett, a Pennsylvanian, tall and strong of arm, was going out with them. Others had various destinations in mind.

Harris Evers, going to rout out his partner, Old Mac, replied to the cheery good mornings of his friends.

Everyone glanced around quickly as there came a shout from the trail down the slope, a side path that curved through heavy chaparral and rocks to join the main road up the Gulch. A couple of big wagons hove into view, the teamsters lashing their mules up the hill into the camp.

"What's all this?" demanded Sam Wilton, of the leading driver, as the panting mules were brought to a stop.

"Compliments of Mayor Tabor and Nevada Charlie, folks," roared the jovial driver. "Help yoreselves!"

They had been low on provisions ever since they had consumed the last of the meat donated by the Rio Kid. He and Bat Masterson had chipped in to supply more, but there were many mouths to feed. The wagon folks needed clothing, too, and other supplies, and they found them in these wagons which had been sent up.

"I reckon," muttered Harris Evers, "we can thank the Rio Kid mostly for all this! Tabor and Nevada Charlie savvy we're his friends!"

Evers located Old Mac, bleary-eyed and with a swollen head from the large amount of raw whiskey he had drunk the night before.

"Get up! We're startin' to find our fortune, Mac," Evers grinned, stirring his partner with his boot toe.

"Ugh," grunted Old Mac, sitting up, licking parched lips, and blinking in the bright sunlight. "What hit me, Harris?"

Evers pulled the old fellow to his feet, gave him some cool water to drink, at the taste of which Old Mac grimaced in disgust. He was still under the influence, but was able to stagger in Evers' wake. Packing their mining tools and a scant bundle of provisions on a horse, the two sang out their farewells to the camp and started across the flat, to scale the nearby ridge and head into the hills. Other small parties of prospectors were already on their way, Sam Wilton among them.

There were more mining camps in the vicinity of Leadville, crude little settlements where a scant living was being scratched from the earth. But none had hit it rich as had the roaring town where Horace Tabor was mayor and principal owner.

Claims were staked all about near Leadville, and Evers and Old Mac had to travel several miles before they found a spot where they could start digging on their own. They soon came upon silver and lead ore but it did not pan out in sufficient quantities to justify staking.

Old Mac was not of much account during the morning, but perked up in the afternoon and did his share. He was an expert cook and could shake up an edible meal from almost nothing. He was familiar with veins and precious minerals, too, and had taught Evers all the young fellow knew about prospecting.

Old Mac and Evers stayed out, hunting all through the daylight hours, sleeping dog-tired and dirty and ill-fed through the darkness. After four days, their provisions ran out entirely, and they were forced to retrace their steps toward the wagon camp, arriving just before darkness set in.

Here they found most of their friends—Sam Wilton, the Smythes, Burnett, Dave Grogan, and the rest. They were all in the same boat. They had failed to strike anything rich in the way of gold, silver or lead, and they had not had sufficient provisions and equipment to maintain an extended search.

There were glum faces among the gathering about the campfire that night. Pike's Peak had proved a hoax. Leadville was true enough, and there were millions there, but they were preempted.

As they were talking the situation over in council, someone rode up on the trail from the town, singing out a cheery good evening. Nevada Charlie, with his white beard and wrinkled pink face, stepped into the circle of ruby light, raising his hand in greeting to the prospectors.

"Hello, boys, howdy!" Charlie cried. "Any luck?"

"No suh," Sam Wilton replied. " 'Pears it ain't so easy to strike it rich in Leadville as they say. But we were shore obleeged to the mayor and you for them wagons of supplies yuh sent."

The faces about him were crestfallen, as Nevada Charlie glanced around. He grinned, waved the thanks aside.

"I reckoned yuh'd find it out for yoreselves by now, 'bout the mines," the white-beard went on. "Yuh see, I savvy Leadville and the camps roundabout. No big strike's ever been made here 'cept in the old canyon itself. Used to call it California Gulch, but now it's Leadville."

"Shucks," growled Fred Smythe. "Yuh couldn't squeeze into that gulch with a shoehorn, Charlie. It's all staked out."

"Uh huh, that's right. Still and all, not every claim in it

47

pays, not the way Tabor's do. Now you folks listen to me. I'm purty old, and I can't go at it and dig the way I used to. I got the Maiden's Prayer, but I ain't sellin' it. She's the best payer in the Gulch. Then I got the Potato Hole—that's up at the far end of the Gulch, not far from here. Dug some there myself last year but my back catches me too bad to try it any more. We skinned off the cream, it's true, and it looks played out. I'm willin' to sell her to yuh folks cheap."

Wilton glanced around at his friends. The miners perked up, interested.

"Sounds all right," Wilton nodded. "Only trouble is, Charlie, we ain't got much cash, not enough to buy a claim in the Gulch."

"Oh, I ain't the kind to drive too hard a bargain," Nevada Charlie replied. "How much can yuh put up?"

Wilton consulted with his friends, while Charlie waited, resting on his stone seat.

"We got twelve hundred dollars between us, all in all," Wilton reported.

"H'm. Ain't much, is it? How 'bout some of them wagons and draught hosses yuh brought here? They'd fetch somethin'."

"That's right. We'll throw them in."

"Well—I dunno. Tell yuh what—I'll sell yuh the claim for that but yuh pay me ten per cent of what comes out. How 'bout it?"

With the air of a man driving a shrewd bargain, Nevada Charlie completed the transaction. The papers would be signed in the morning, and legally executed.

Then Nevada Charlie took his leave, and the prospectors began discussing the purchase of the new claim. Some were dubious about the advisability of putting their last dollars into a mine which was admittedly "played out."

"That Nevada Charlie ain't no sucklin' babe," Ed Young declared. "They say he's got a million dollars tucked away, and he knows more of minin' than all of us put together. Why should he sell us a valuable piece of property for a few hundred?"

Harris Evers had listened to the talk. He, too, was puzzled at Nevada Charlie's action.

"I wonder," he mused to himself, "if it's on account of the Rio Kid?"

He had been present when Nevada Charlie had offered to give Pryor a silver claim up the gulch, after the Rio Kid had bulldozed Olsen and Smothers. He had guessed that the presents sent up by Tabor and Charlie had been thanks to Pryor.

"What we got to lose?" said Sam Wilton. "All our cash'll be gone soon, anyways, if we don't strike quick. The cost of livin' up here's enough to bankrupt the U.S. Mint. I vote we hop into it."

"Me, too!" Evers cried.

Enthusiasm seized on them, and the vote was aye.

In the morning, representatives of the prospectors—Sam Wilton, Evers, the Smythes and several others—hurried into Leadville and met Nevada Charlie. The deal was consummated and initial payment made.

"I hope yuh never regret it, gents." Charlie smiled. "Just keep a-diggin' that's my advice."

Hurrying back, they broke camp, and moved closer to the well-marked, but small area in the Gulch which now was theirs. Big chunks had been dug out of the rock, the irregular pattern showing how the top vein ran.

Having no machinery, it was necessary to do the work by hand. Old Mac, Sam Wilton and other elders expert in mining and supervised the operations. Picks and shovels, as well as screens were manipulated, and drills were ready as they prepared to cut into the rock, to hunt for another vein.

Evers worked cheerfully, his powerful young muscles a great help. Old Mac knew how to wield the tools, and despite his age could stand up with the best.

They took out nothing but rock that day. Worn out at nightfall, with the surrounding sounds from the bigger mines and machinery in their ears, they retired to their little camp and ate what the women had prepared.

Evers kept a wary eye on Old Mac. He was fond of his partner, and wanted to hold Mac to the straight and narrow for a time, until they had accumulated a little surplus, at least. This was difficult, because when near a town and an unfailing supply of whiskey, Old Mac could not long resist its call.

For a couple of days after their lucky start, thanks to Nevada Charlie, Old Mac behaved like a lamb, but one evening Evers noted the signs of restlessness in his friend. Old Mac didn't eat much and he kept involuntarily glancing down toward Leadville with its garish array of shacks and buildings.

Light blazed to the sky from hundreds of lamps in town, and they could hear the distant, sinister hum of many coarse voices. Miners were whooping it up after a day of toil in the various claims.

"Don't do it, Mac," begged Evers. "Hold yore thirst, for my sake. After all, we got a fine chance here. Yuh said yoreself there was signs there may be a second vein underneath."

"All right, boy," Old Mac promised and licked his parched lips, again looking toward Leadville.

Dorothy Wilton had avoided Evers as much as possible since their talk. When they chanced to come face to face, she would nod to him and drop her eyes, but there always seemed to be someone else near and she made no opportunities for him to speak privately with her.

Harris was working from dawn till dusk, and at night she was usually with her father or in the rough canvas and brush shack which Sam Wilton had built.

After the evening meal, Evers made ready to turn in. He simply had to roll in his blanket and lie down under a bush. He saw to it that Old Mac was beside him, and even before Evers drifted off, Old Mac was snoring loudly.

When he awoke Evers knew by the stars, as he looked up into the dome of the sky, that it was around midnight.

The camp was dark and quiet, and snores reached his listening ears. There was also the shrill piping of insects and night birds, with the always present wolfish noise made by Leadville a mile away down the Gulch.

Evers did not catch his partner's stertorous breathing in his ear, however, and putting out his hand, he felt the blanket which had wrapped Old Mac, but it had no body in it. Some stones held it out in the rough shape of a man, but Old Mac was gone.

"Doggone him," muttered Evers, sitting up. "He's so danged crafty, or thinks he is, the old goat!"

He was angry. Old Mac would be no good for anything for several days if he really got liquored up. Sometimes Mac would stay that way for a week.

However, Mac had not had any money, but Evers remembered having seen him talking to a party of dudes who had come to see the sights of Leadville and had wandered up the Gulch. He might well have talked them out of enough to start assuaging his raging thirst.

The criticism Dorothy Wilton had voiced of his partner had stung Evers. He wanted to have her see how fine Mac was at heart, and to know that the old fellow could work hard and long if he wished to. This dereliction would prove she was right.

Evers rose. "I'll go get him 'fore he really warms up," he decided.

Pulling on his boots and hat, Evers silently left the sleeping camp, taking the path down the Gulch to Leadville.

The night life of the town was wild and furious. It was dangerous as well. A man with any wealth on him was not safe roaming the streets after dark. Holdups were common, and death no surprise in Leadville.

Evers was not worried, however. He had no cash to speak of and his clothing was old. Moreover, he wore a six-shooter in his belt.

Many saloons were wide open, despite the hour, and he hurried along Harrison Avenue, pausing to glance in at the lines of men at each bar.

51

"State Street's more Mac's line, I reckon," Evers thought, swinging through a narrow side street.

On State were the cheaper, and more vicious dives. Old Mac's pocketbook would send him to spots where drinks cost least.

Coming into State Street, lined with the squalid dives, Evers saw Bull Olsen emerge from Dinty's, the place where the Rio Kid had bluffed and out-shot Smothers and his bunch. Olsen walked unsteadily along the high board sidewalk, away from Evers, who crossed the rutted road to the other side.

Harris Evers had no intention of having his search for his partner interfered with.

CHAPTER VII

Nevada Charlie Passes

☐ Old Mac was not in Dinty's or in any of the places on that side. Evers then crossed back. There was a small saloon that was labeled. "Tex's" near the next corner and he headed for it. Sure enough, as he stepped up on the high porch from the wooden walk, he saw Old Mac sagging on the bar in the back of the narrow room.

He hit the batwings and hurried in. Old Mac, turning bleary eyes that way, saw him coming. Shame and surprise lit the prospector's face for a moment. He turned and, partly sobered by the shock of seeing his angry partner's young face, ran from the saloon through the back door.

"Wait, Mac!" Evers called, taking after him.

The back door stood open. Evers listened and, hearing the progress of his friend up the dark alley that was crowded with tin cans and garbage piles, swung left to trail Mac.

Old Mac didn't get far. He passed a couple of windows from which feeble shafts of light shone, placing him for Evers. Then, in his half-sodden condition, he tripped on a stone and fell flat on his face, remaining there.

When Evers came up with him Old Mac was breathing heavily, and the red-eye had him down. Evers turned

53

him over, shook him, but Old Mac was either out or playing possum.

"Dang yuh!" muttered Evers, "I ought to spank you, Mac."

Suddenly Evers glanced up. He had heard a muffled gunshot, not far away, from the back of a darkened small house which fronted on Harrison Avenue. The alley gave light and air to the rows of houses back against each other on the two main thoroughfares of Leadville.

Stooping beside Old Mac, and in the shadows of a pile of refuse, Evers caught hurried sounds. A man climbed from the darkened open window of the dwelling. He looked back as he passed through the light shaft from a dive's back door, and Evers recognized Bull Olsen. Then the big Swede was gone.

Puzzled, Evers straightened up, and walked to the window from which Olsen had come so quickly. He looked in, but the room was dark. Then he heard a low moan.

" 'Tain't none of my business," he thought, striking a match, "but—"

The little flare showed some of the room. A man lay on a bunk along the wall. The flame caught the white beard and with a shock Evers realized it *was* his business, for the man was Nevada Charlie.

He dived inside, and struck another match. The slight little figure lay quiet. There were dark stains of blood on his beard, blood that welled from his lips. His eyes were staring. He had a bullet-hole through the jut of his chin. The slug which had ranged upward probably had lodged in or close to his brain.

As Evers bent over him, Charlie whispered:

"Bull—"

"It was Olsen—I seen him," Evers growled. "Wait'll I call the sawbones."

But he knew it was useless. Even as he spoke, Nevada Charlie shuddered, flexed, and relaxed. He was dead.

"There'll be the devil and all to pay," Evers muttered, "when the Rio Kid rides back!"

He did not know, though, that even then the Rio Kid

was nearing Leadville and that before many hours he would be seen in its streets.

Early the next evening the Rio Kid, with his partners, Bat Masterson and Celestino Mireles, rode into the park outside Leadville. The wagons laden with supplies were coming in behind them.

"That was a good trip, Rio Kid," Bat declared, pleased. "We made plenty!"

Well satisfied with the big wages they had earned for their trouble, and thirsting for a drink and hot meal after the trail, the trio headed into town and toward the biggest, fanciest restaurant Leadville could boast.

The sun was red behind the mighty Rockies rearing their snow-crested heads about the high settlement. Leadville was humming its usual wicked tune. Already lights were blinking on in the saloons and other places of amusement, as the three returned gun guards sat down to fill up.

They had about finished a fully appreciated meal when Horace Tabor, mayor and first citizen of Leadville, entered the place. A broad smile was on his face, his great waxed mustache was twisted up jauntily, and as usual he was surrounded by sycophants.

He nodded to the Rio Kid and his friends, waving a fat hand that sparkled with big diamonds in golden circlets.

The best table, in the brightest corner, had been reserved for Tabor, and pretty young women hurried over to join his party. Champagne was brought in, and the most expensive delicacies served at the mayor's table.

The Rio Kid watched, amused at Tabor's florid enjoyment of his wealth. The head man of Leadville loved the limelight and loved to mix. He was childish in this, basking in the public eye.

While the trio who had finished eating were lighting up cigars at the end of their meal, Mireles said softly:

"General, here ees Evers!"

The Rio Kid glanced at the front entry as Harris Evers came in and crossed toward their table.

"Howdy, Evers," sang out Pryor.

"Hullo, Rio Kid," Evers said, shaking hands. "Mighty glad yuh're back."

He greeted Bat Masterson and the Mexican youth, and turned a sober face to the Rio Kid as he sat down.

"How yuh gettin' along?" Pryor inquired. "Strike it rich yet Evers?"

To his astonishment, Evers nodded.

"Yeah, I think so."

"Well, dang my hide!" exclaimed the Rio Kid. "Yuh *think* so?"

"We ain't altogether shore yet," explained Evers. "But late this afternoon we uncovered a silver and lead vein that looks mighty promisin'."

"Where?"

"At our mine, up at the end of the Gulch."

"Where'd yuh get a mine from?" demanded Masterson.

"Nevada Charlie sold it to us 'fore he died."

The Rio Kid jumped, frowned.

"What'd yuh say, Evers?"

"Nevada Charlie sold us a claim up the Gulch, cheap." He stared into the Rio Kid's stern face. "Yeah, I savvy why he done it, though not all of 'em realize it. It was because we're friends of yores, Rio Kid, and Charlie wanted to give us a hand. Yuh wouldn't take any reward for savin' his life, so he done it this way. At least, that's how I figger it."

"How'd he die?" growled Pryor.

"His body was found in his bed at home this mornin'. He was shot through the head."

"Who done it?"

Evers glanced around, lowered his voice.

"I've kept my trap shut, Rio Kid. Didn't tell anybody. But last night I was huntin' Old Mac, who was on a bust, and I was in the alley back of Charlie's place. I heard a muffled shot, and seen a man climb out of Charlie's winder. When I went in, Charlie was dyin'."

The Rio Kid's anger was mounting. Under his heavy tan, the blood was darkening his cheeks. His hands,

56

trained to the six-shooter, were twitching slightly and he had a tense look as he listened to Evers' story.

"Who was the man?"

"It was Bull Olsen. He was drunk."

"Yuh ain't told anybody 'bout this?"

Evers shook his head. "I reckoned it was better to wait till you got back. If I'd shot off my mouth, it might have meant trouble for all the folks in camp."

"That was a smart play."

The Rio Kid stood up, pushing back his chair. His slim hands caressed the Army Colts as he tested them without looking at them, by sense of touch, making sure they would not drag in the holsters, that they were loaded.

"I'll go over to Dinty's with yuh, Rio Kid," Bat Masterson said softly, also rising.

Mireles said nothing. There was no need for him to speak because he was always ready to back up his partner of the wild trails.

Harris Evers was armed, gun in the belt circling his narrow hips.

"Take me, too, Rio Kid," he begged. "It's my fight. You got into this on account of helpin' us."

The Rio Kid stalked toward the front door, his three comrades trailing at his heels. As he passed near Tabor's table, the sound of feminine laughter and masculine guffaws grew louder. Corks were popping, and everybody was having a fine time.

"Rio Kid!" Horace Tabor hailed him jovially. "Stop and toast the ladies!"

The Rio Kid swung, pausing beside the big man. The young women looked up at the handsome, stern features of the lithe Rio Kid, admiration in their bright eyes.

The Rio Kid accepted the glass of champagne and, with his friends, drank the toast. Deliberately he set the thin-stemmed glass down on the nearby table.

"Nevada Charlie's dead, I hear," he said to the mayor in a low voice.

Tabor stopped laughing. "Yeah, pore feller. Found

him dead in bed this mornin'. Duggan's workin' on it. 'Pears to be a great mystery who kilt him."

"It ain't to me," the Rio Kid told him softly.

Tabor pinned the Rio Kid with his eyes.

"When I saw yuh eatin' and drinkin' in here," he said deliberately, "I figgered yuh just didn't give a hang, and it surprised me, to say the least. Thought I savvied yuh better than that. Yuh just found it out. I know yuh guaranteed Charlie's life." He paused and added in a low voice, "Olsen and his mates are bad medicine. Yuh've been away and while yuh been gone they ain't let the grass grow under their feet. They're crowdin' us, Rio Kid. I feel it in my marrow."

"I'm still a special deputy?"

"Yuh're still a special deputy."

The Rio Kid's pride was smarting. He had guaranteed Nevada Charlie's life, and Bull Olsen had dared flaunt the challenge in his face for all Leadville to see. The Rio Kid's reputation on the Frontier was in danger, for everybody had heard how he had run Olsen into his hole and made Bull pull the cover on.

He was not yet aware why Olsen and Smothers had picked out Nevada Charlie to destroy and rob. Though he had seen them try to jump Charlie's big town lot the first day he, the Rio Kid, had been in Leadville.

With a short nod, the Rio Kid was on his way. He left the Giltedge, stalking the high boardwalks and on past the lighted windows of the gay places on Harrison Avenue. Miners jostled him in the street, oblivious to the undercurrents of conflict in Leadville that did not directly affect them. It was every man for himself there.

Bat Masterson walked with the Rio Kid, while Mireles and Evers brought up the rear, all four girded for action.

Pryor turned the next corner, through Cross Street, leading to State Street on which stood Dinty's and other low dives.

"Listen here, Rio Kid," suggested Masterson softly, "let's not go off half-cocked. Strategy counts, don't it? If

58

Olsen killed Nevada Charlie, they'll be on guard and watchin' for us. Ain't it so?"

"That's so," the Rio Kid agreed, but he had no intention of walking into an ambush.

"There goes Turkey Craw!" Evers suddenly discovered.

The quartet had paused at the corner, looking down the sweep of State Street. The gawky Turkey Craw, the thief who had traveled to Colorado with the decent prospectors, hurried up the walk and swung into Dinty's, where Bull Olsen and George Smothers had their headquarters.

"He must've seen us, when we came outa the restaurant," figured the Rio Kid. "Reckon he was watchin' for me, boys. Is that dirty horse-thief spyin' for Olsen now?"

"Wouldn't surprise me a bit," Evers growled. "He quit us soon as we hit Leadville, and he hates yore insides, Rio Kid. He ain't got the nerve to buck yuh head-on, but he's just the sort who would spy for a bunch like Smothers runs."

The Rio Kid nodded. If Turkey Craw warned Olsen and Smothers he was coming, then direct assault would be much more difficult.

"It means they got guilty consciences," he said musingly. "They killed Nevada Charlie—no doubt of it."

"They say Olsen's been enlistin' more men for Smothers," remarked Evers.

"We'll watch for a few minutes and see what stirs," ordered Bob Pryor, the Rio Kid.

They crossed over the side street and waited in the shadows. A few minutes after Turkey Craw had disappeared inside Dinty's, several men wearing guns hastily came from the saloon and posted themselves at both sides of the entrance.

"They'll have gunnies swarmin' in the alleys and halls, shore as yuh're born," growled the Rio Kid. "Olsen and Smothers'll be covered like turtles."

"S'ppose I ride up to camp and fetch some of our boys," suggested Evers.

The Rio Kid shook his head. "No. I don't want to get 'em mixed up in this, Evers. Most of 'em are family men and some would be shore to be hurt."

"Hey—here comes Marty Duggan!" warned Bat Masterson. "He'll horn in and try to spile our fun. That's his job."

CHAPTER VIII

Gunfight

☐ Duggan, the marshal, with holster belts flapping about his sturdy legs, came galloping over from Harrison Avenue, no doubt warned that trouble was brewing. The Rio Kid and his friends drew back, hidden in the blackness at the side of a darkened shack on the cross streets.

Duggan hurried to Dinty's, and went inside.

"He'll soon get tired of waitin'," observed Pryor. "Duggan's all right, but he'll check us for law and order. Let's start, boys. I got an idea."

The three men with him trailed after him to the evil-odored back alley, and he worked through the cluttered yards till they were behind the line of buildings on State Street. The buildings were chiefly of one story, with false fronts on the street. Though here and there a two-storied place reared up.

The Rio Kid and his loyal comrades soon found a water pipe, which drained rain off the slanting roof of a house near the corner. He shinned up it, got hold of the gutter, and pulled himself to the roof. Giving a hand to the others, he helped them reach the roof. There they found that save for a few narrow gaps and a couple of ten-foot house walls interposing, they had a route overhead that would take them straight to Dinty's.

"This is the stuff!" exclaimed Bat Masterson, catching the Rio Kid's idea. "We can get right to Olsen's winder over the roofs!"

Slowly, making few sounds that were not drowned in the usual wolfish howls of the wicked town, the Rio Kid's revenge party started for Dinty's. They used much the same methods to reach higher roofs, boosting the Rio Kid up first, where he could lean down and give a hand to the rest. Luckily most of the roofs extended out beyond the walls, to protect the windows below from drip, and none of the narrow gaps between buildings proved too wide a jump.

Dinty's sprawling, mud-chinked log joint was a single-story building. When they reached it they tiptoed over to the west side, aware from their previous visit of the location of the private room in which Bull Olsen and George Smothers usually sat.

"Keep down and stay quiet till I reconnoiter, boys," whispered the Rio Kid.

He dropped down on all fours and hunched toward the edge of the roof. Below were the lighted windows, while the *stamp-stamp* of dancing feet, the raucous cries of hilarious miners, and tinny music shook the place.

The Rio Kid located the windows he wanted. They were open. Tobacco smoke drifted up, fresh puffs of it. Peeking over the overhang, the Rio Kid saw the red glow of a cigar as a man standing in the narrow alleyway at the side of Dinty's drew on his cheroot. Toward the street he now glimpsed more dark figures, and the glint of gunmetal caught by light-shafts from the window openings.

Silent, flat on his belly, the Rio Kid waited. After a while a man stuck his head and shoulders from one of the back parlor windows.

"Hey, Barry," he asked in a tense voice, "see anything yet?"

The man with the cigar turned toward the window.

"Nope," he growled. "Nary hide nor hair, Bull."

"Cuss it all!" complained Olsen, "I wish he'd come and

get it over with. I got my men all set. Why in tarnation did he have to come back to Leadville anyhow?"

"We'll fill him full of lead, Bull," growled Barry, patting his Colt. "That Rio Kid's as good as planted."

Ears strained, the Rio Kid caught another voice, as a man behind Bull spoke from inside the room.

"Pull yourself together, Olsen. You brought this on us. I wasn't quite ready, but I suppose we must go on with it now."

"Shucks, Chief," remonstrated Olsen. "It wasn't too soon to get rid of Nevada Charlie. With him outa the way, we can hop in and grab what we need, can't we? I figgered the Rio Kid wasn't comin' back a-tall, and even if he did what proof would he have that I done it? What proof's he got now? Anyways, he'll walk into my trap, see if he don't, and that'll settle the whole matter. We can wipe them other fools out any time, with Wilton and Evers off the map."

It was about twelve feet to the beaten dirt alley running alongside Dinty's log wall. The Rio Kid gauged it carefully. He inched back, raising his arm so his friends, back on the roof, could see his signal.

"Here we go," he muttered.

Olsen had just drawn in his head and shoulders as the Rio Kid landed in the alley, and with pistol in hand doubled up. Lithe as a panther in his youthful strength, his surprise was complete. Barry, at the corner, could not shoot instantly when the Rio Kid came up straight. For one thing, Barry was slow. For another, Olsen and Smothers had reached the window almost instantly, and the gunny's bullets would have lashed them.

To cover his flank, the Rio Kid sent a snap shot at Barry, and the man's cigar described an arc through the air. The slug had hit Barry in the chin. It bowled him over.

A moment later Bat Masterson landed in the alley, then came Mireles and Evers, just as the Rio Kid threw himself over the windowsill into the private room. The astounded Bull Olsen, with the opening gunshot sharp in his flapping ears, did not understand what had occurred until he saw the Rio Kid straighten up before him.

"The Rio Kid!"

That shout came from Squirrel Hart, Smothers' little aide. Hart had been sitting in a chair near the door, an old flint-lock rifle leaning against the wall between himself and one of Smothers' husky gun guards. The black eyes of Smothers, just behind Bull Olsen, widened, then began blinking furiously. The Rio Kid caught the flash of sudden alarm in Smothers' eyes, but the stern gaze of Bob Pryor was on Olsen, the huge Swede.

"Yuh killed Nevada Charlie, Olsen, after my warnin'," the Rio Kid announced coldly. There was a little smile on his lips.

"No, I didn't!" stammered Bull. "That's a lie!"

The Rio Kid stared with stern accusation into the big man's flat, scared face. Olsen was fishy under his tan. His huge hands were shaking at his sides, and he trembled all over, apparently forgetful of the Colts he wore at either hip.

There were four other members of the gang in the private room huddled together on the right of the Rio Kid as he faced the gathering.

Harris Evers was only a moment or two behind the Rio Kid as he climbed through the window, and Mireles came next. Masterson, covering the alley, crouched just outside, two guns in hand, ready for fight.

"I saw yuh come out of Charlie's room that night, Olsen!' shouted Evers angrily. "Yuh murdered him in his sleep!"

"Yuh lie!" slobbered Olsen. "That ain't so—I never was near the place! Rio Kid—for mercy's sake, don't—"

"Draw, yuh onery sidewinder!" snarled the Rio Kid. "I warned yuh what'd happen if yuh hurt Nevada Charlie!"

Mireles gave a quick Spanish oath as he leaped into the room, and something flashed in the lamplight as the Mexican's long knife, appearing like magic from the leg of his velvet pants, flew across the room. He had seen the movement of the gunny bodyguard. The fellow yelled, as the sharp blade cut his arm. The old rifle he had grabbed exploded, the charge ripping above Mireles' head. The guard dropped the gun and, with blood spurting from his cut, lunged through the door.

In a panic of fear, Bull Olsen dropped a big hand to a Colt butt, started his gun clearing leather. The Rio Kid let him begin—and beat him to it. Olsen's revolver roared, the echoes loud in the confined space of the room. The bullet kicked splinters from the rough flooring near the Rio Kid's spread feet. Then a bluish hole showed between Olsen's baby-blue eyes, and the fear on his flat face was replaced by wonder.

The giant gunman began to teeter, and slowly folded up where he stood, in a limp heap, his gun clattering to the floor beside him.

"Kill him, you fools!" That was George Smothers, cursing the paralyzed gunnies standing in a huddle.

Obeying their chief's order, they dug for their irons. The Rio Kid swung on them just as Evers shot, getting a man in the shoulder. Then the Rio Kid's blazing Colts tore at the bunched gang, and two more men went down, riddled in as many counts.

Slugs came at the trio. Out in the alley, Bat Masterson's pistols blazed their song of death, as the doughty Bat cleaned the narrow way of gunnies seeking to get in.

Shrieks, curses, the bellowing of heavy revolvers filled the room where the main gun fight was going on.

George Smothers, moving with astonishing speed, ducked behind the big-topped table in the middle of the room. On it stood the lamp, and Smothers overturned the table, spilling poker chips, cards, glasses, whiskey bottle, and the lamp itself, to the floor.

The light flicked out as the hot chimney smashed. Kerosene doused the little flame and bluish-yellow stabs of exploding powder exposed for instants the set faces of the fighting men.

From the corner where men making a stand had been ripped by the lead of the Rio Kid and his two friends, only one gun was sending back reply shots. The others had been stilled, and after a couple of shots the last gun quit.

"Cover the door!" shouted Pryor, leaping that way.

A bullet burned his cheek with a kiss of death, but luckily missing save for the singe on his skin. It came from the doorway leading into the hall. A man showed against the dim light outside the door, and the Rio Kid, thinking it was Smothers shooting sent two bullets into the man in the door. He pitched forward and lay still, with his legs in the private room and his shoulders outside it.

"Hey, Rio Kid, it's hot out here!" shouted Bat Masterson, and dived in the open window. "Can I come in?"

Most of Olsen's guards had been posted along the approaches to Dinty's, watching for an attack from the street. They hadn't thought of the route across the roofs, taken by the Rio Kid and his aides.

"C'mon, Bat," called the Rio Kid, pausing at the door as he saw Masterson leap through the window. "There is still more to do!"

Dead and wounded men remained in the private room. Heavy footsteps, running up the hall, sent the Rio Kid that way. He looked up toward the main saloon, and glimpsed George Smothers as the big man flashed around the turn at the swinging door. Smothers passed Marshal Marty Duggan as the lawman came charging through from the front of the saloon.

"Hey, what in thunder's goin' on back there?" roared Duggan.

"Stay back, Duggan!" warned the Rio Kid.

But Duggan kept coming. The Rio Kid hesitated. He would not shoot it out with the law. But even as he paused a bullet ripped through Masterson's shirt, and Bat cursed, turned and fired at the open windows. Olsen's sentries were coming in, thick and fast, to get into the scrap.

Marty Duggan slid to a stop, brandishing his gun.

"Yuh fool!" he snarled, reaching for the Rio Kid. "I

don't give a hoot if yuh are a special depitty, I'll have yore hide!"

Slugs were tearing through the window as Olsen's gang opened fire. The Rio Kid jumped aside, but Duggan caught a bullet in the left forearm. Shrieking and cursing, Marty Duggan began shooting at the windows, at the dark forms bunched outside in the alley.

Grinning, the Rio Kid joined the marshal, as did Masterson, Evers and Celestino Mireles.

"Yuh see, Marshal?" called Pryor, over the crashing guns. "It's the only language they savvy!"

The accuracy of the crack marksmen inside the room quickly discouraged the hirelings outside. Several felt the lead thrown at them. The ones in back quit pushing, and turned to sneak away.

As the heavy revolvers ceased their snarling uproar, the ringing ears of the men began to distinguish the yells of the startled people in Dinty's saloon. Powder-smoke drifted acrid to the ceiling, filling the air.

"Strike a match, cuss it!" bawled Marty Duggan.

Bat Masterson obliged. He found a candle on a shelf, and lighted it. Duggan, scowling at the Rio Kid, turned and counted the dead.

He stooped over Bull Olsen, who was sprawled on the floor. Two other gunnies were lifeless in a corner, and another was groaning on the floor, with a torn side. In the hall lay the fourth of the guards who had been in the room with Olsen, Hart and Smothers.

Duggan counted them. Then he looked out the window, and counted several more outside, wounded and killed.

The Rio Kid took a chair, and lit up a smoke. His friends clustered about him, slapping him on the back. In the doorway, the alarmed faces of Dinty, owner of the place, and of some of his customers showed. The hall was rapidly filling with people as the fight ended.

"About fifteen, dead or wounded, I'd say," growled Marty Duggan, frowning at the Rio Kid! "How many of you gun-slingin' fools was there?"

"Just us four," Masterson replied.

"Cuss it," Duggan said, "I knowed yuh'd come over here. How'd yuh get in without me seein' yuh?"

"That's a perfessional secret, Duggan," the Rio Kid grinned.

Mayor Horace Tabor came shouldering through the crowd. He had been summoned by a frightened citizen.

"What goes on here?" the big man cried. "Rio Kid! So yuh made it!"

His pop eyes swung, viewing the carnage, took in Bull Olsen and the others.

"There's more outside, Tabor," Duggan growled and swore.

"What yuh got to say for yoreself, Rio Kid?" Tabor demanded.

The Rio Kid shrugged. "Tabor, Harris Evers seen Bull Olsen kill Nevada Charlie, an old friend of mine. I come over here to chide Bull and I'll be blowed if he didn't pull a gun and start at me. That's all."

Suddenly Tabor grinned; then he began to laugh. He laughed until the tears rolled down his fat cheeks and dripped off the waxed ends of his preposterous mustache.

He slapped the Rio Kid on the back.

"Come along with me," he ordered.

The Rio Kid winked at Bat Masterson and, trailing the big mayor of Leadville, left the excited crowd in Dinty's. Bat Masterson, Celestino, and Evers followed in the wake of the crowd which swarmed along after the now famous Rio Kid, whose gunfighting ability had become known.

The number of those dead by the guns of Pryor, Masterson and the other two partners swelled to a prodigious score, increasing with each recounting.

CHAPTER IX

Bodyguard

☐ Glorifying in the prowess of the Rio Kid Mayor Tabor led Pryor over to the Giltedge and into the saloon, bawling for way in his loud voice.

As they went to the rear of the big place, a man stood up, singing out a greeting to Tabor. The mayor paused.

"Why, George!" he exclaieed. "When'd you pull in?"

"This afternoon, Horace. Thought I'd stop off and see how the old town is boomin'."

Tabor introduced the Rio Kid.

"George, this here is Bob Pryor, called the Rio Kid. Rio Kid, shake with George Pullman, one of the Gulch's first prospectors. Made a nice stake up Gregory Gulch. Yuh still foolin' with them cars, George?"

Pullman smiled. "I sure am, Horace."

Tabor laughed heartily. "George was hipped on inventin' a fancy car he calls after hisself, a 'Pullman'! Yuh let down a shelf and sleep on the seats. If that ain't a funny one!"

The Rio Kid smiled. "Why, it mightn't be so bad, Tabor. A man could sleep acrost the kentry and be fresh when he got where he was goin'."

"Yeah," objected Tabor, "but it costs money. Who's goin' to pay extra money to lay down on a train when they can just as well sleep in the seats?"

"They're doing it, Horace," Pullman said, laughing.

Tabor nodded and went on. He led the Rio Kid to a private parlor in the rear, where an obsequious waiter hurried to fill their orders.

"I want to talk turkey, Rio Kid," began Tabor, when they were alone. "I've heard a lot about you and noted how yuh have behaved here in Leadville. Yuh ain't what I'd call a quiet, retirin' sort, but in such a wild town men like yuh're needed. Yuh've hurt nobody decent. Yore guns have fired only on scum like Bull Olsen and his gang. Fact is, I like yuh. Yuh're a man after my own heart, and I want yuh to work for me."

Tabor beamed, lifting his frosted glass to drink to the Rio Kid.

"How so, Mayor?" inquired the Rio Kid curiously. "What's yore proposition?"

Tabor wiped his great mustache with the back of a hairy hand that sparkled with diamonds, and leaned forward confidentially.

"I got political aspersions, between you and me, Rio Kid. I'm goin' to be governor when Colorado is admitted to statehood, and after that I'm goin' to Washington as United States Senator!"

Horace Tabor leaned back in his chair as though he had just delivered a bombshell, watching the effect on the Rio Kid.

"Where do I come in?" asked Bob Pryor, secretly amused at Tabor's manner.

"I'm startin' for Denver, and then goin' on to Washin'ton to see what I can do about workin' for Colorado statehood in a couple of days," explained Tabor, "and I want you to travel with me, Rio Kid. Officially yuh'll be my bodyguard, savvy? It will make a big stir in the East to have yuh struttin' along beside me, won't it, dressed fit to kill and wearin' yore guns?"

For a moment, the Rio Kid felt that he must refuse. Then he nodded. It would be amusing, and he would see plenty of excitement, following Horace Tabor's flamboyant trail.

"I'll go, if I can first make shore Smothers and the rest of Olsen's pards are on the run, Mayor. Young Evers may be in danger from 'em. He's already spoilt Smothers' game in Leadville and is responsible for the fun we had tonight, since he saw Olsen murder Nevada Charlie. Fact is, Smothers hates all that bunch of wagon train folks, and if I savvy that kind of snake, he'll take a stab at gettin' even. Smothers and his gang was after Charlie's wealth, but now—"

Tabor shrugged. "Main reason I can leave now is thanks to yore work tonight, Rio Kid. I been afeared to leave Leadville with Olsen and that Smothers sidewinder kickin' up their heels. Now yuh've settled their hash and I don't figger they'll come back here after tonight."

The Rio Kid finished his drink, then left the mayor. He found his cronies waiting in the main bar for him, and they went out on the street. With the Rio Kid in the lead, they began to patrol slowly through Leadville.

The first place the Rio Kid headed for was State Street and Dinty's. He went inside, and there was a sudden silence, gasps as he was recognized. Men pointed him out and nodded to him. They were chiefly admiring, for his fame had skyrocketed after the big fight.

There was no trouble at all, for the Rio Kid. The survivors of Olsen's gang, as well as George Smothers, Squirrel Hart and the rest of Smothers' gunnies were out of sight.

Finally the friends turned in to sleep, back at the camp.

In the morning, the Rio Kid rose, cleaned up, as spruce as usual, and ate breakfast. Then saddling Saber, he started for town. He meant to keep his eye peeled for signs of Smothers, but the sunny day was peaceful and he saw none of the gunmen about Leadville.

Later in the morning, Bat Masterson and Celestino Mireles, who had been circulating about just as the Rio Kid had, joined him at the corner of Harrison and Main.

"I hear that Smothers, Hart and the whole passel of 'em rode out of town last night, and they say it's for good," reported Bat.

Mireles nodded. "*Si.* So zey say, General. You have bluff zem out."

"Huh—hope so, for Evers' sake, anyways," muttered the Rio Kid, and glanced up the street. "Now what the devil is that bunch up to, with the mayor?"

Tabor, resplendent in morning coat, striped pants and a silk hat; came down the sidewalk, carrying with him a double-barreled shotgun.

"Hi-yuh, Rio Kid!" sang out the mayor in his loud voice. "Join us, will you?"

The Rio Kid fell in with the dozen prominent citizens solemnly parading along Harrison Avenue.

"What's up?" the Rio Kid inquired.

"We just got word a mighty promernint U. S. citizen is on his way to Leadville," replied the mayor. "Name of Horace Greeley. Ever hear tell of him?"

"Yuh mean the newspaper feller from New York—what's the name of that paper of his?"

"That's him." Tabor consulted a paper from his pocket. "*Tribune*, that's his."

The Rio Kid tagged along with the delegation until they reached the outskirts of the town. Up the Gulch were the big mines of Leadville, where men were swarming in the dirt like ants.

"This is far enough, Horace," said a puffing, stout councilman. "Nobody will want to go 'way off. It's too dry."

"All right," agreed Tabor.

He picked a bit of bare dirt and, raising the shotgun fired both barrels into a spot. Turning away as though he had accomplished a great mission, the mayor nodded.

"Let's retire to the Giltedge, gents. I need stimulation."

The mystified Rio Kid waited for an explanation, but none was offered.

"What's the idea, Mayor?" he demanded, as they hurried back into Leadville.

"Huh? What yuh mean?"

"Why'd yuh shoot that buckshot into the earth?"

72

"Oh—why, yuh savvy how these newspaper fellers are," explained Tabor. "Yuh got to show 'em, that's all. We don't want to disappoint Greeley, do we? That wasn't buckshot, it was gold and silver in them shells. Yuh'll see this afternoon." In a low voice he added, "Told yuh yuh'd done the trick! Olsen and Smothers faded!"

After lunch, three men rode into Leadville on mules, from the steep trail to the outer world. One was Horace Greeley, the great newspaper editor, and the Rio Kid joined in the throng which came out to greet him. Mayor Tabor, clad in elegant dress, did the honors in his loud, florid way.

Greeley was getting along in years. The Rio Kid stared at his odd get-up. The editor, puffing in the rarefied air, and from the hard ride, had a pink, baby face fringed by white throat whiskers. He wore a broad-brimmed black hat, a white overcoat, shapeless trousers, and white sox. His eyes blinked in the bright sunlight, as he shook hands all around.

Eccentric, absent-minded, Greeley was a national figure, a political leader as well as a great editor. He had brought his *Tribune* to the top of the crest, made it a power in the land.

"How do you do, sir," Greeley greeted the mayor in his squeaky voice. "I have come to Leadville to see for myself if the stories of its fabulous wealth be true. My readers have a right to know."

"Yuh've come to the right place, hombre!" a citizen shouted.

After refreshments, the Rio Kid, hanging along with Tabor and Greeley, heard the editor say in his high-pitched voice:

"Could you show me some of the precious metals of which stories have reached the civilized world, sir?"

"Shore as shootin', Greeley," cried Tabor, clapping the editor on the back. "Foller me. Jed, fetch that pan and them tools. C'mon—this way."

Everybody trooped after Tabor and Greeley, as the editor was steered to the spot in the hillside of the canyon where the shotgun had been discharged that morning.

"Why, say, there's a likely lookin' spot," exclaimed Tabor, seizing Greeley's arm. "Try diggin' there, Mr. Greeley. Fact is, 'most anywhere yuh dig in Leadville yuh strike metal."

A short-handled miner's pick was shoved into Greeley's hand. Men grouped around as he laboriously dug out some dirt.

"Got to pan it," Tabor said. "Lemme show yuh how it's done."

Water was ready in pails. Horace Greeley inexpertly washed off the dirt from the pebbles and, sure enough, among them could be seen particles of gleaming gold and silver.

Greeley straightened up with a grimace.

"I believe it, for I have seen it with my own eyes! Leadville is rich as the mines of the Pharaohs. If a young man should ask my advice on his career, I should say to him, 'Go West, young man, go West'!"

"Let's all have a drink on me!" Tabor bawled.

While they were refreshing themselves after the hard labor of prospecting, Harris Evers rushed breathlessly into the Giltedge to which they had returned. He stopped beside his friend, the Rio Kid.

"Rio Kid! Rio Kid!" he shrieked. "We've struck it rich! We've hit it!"

"What?" demanded Tabor, turning.

"We've hit the main second vein! It's a yard wide and a mile deep! Worth a million dollars!"

Evers was in the throes of the highest excitement.

"I'll bet Nevada Charlie knowed that vein was there," was Pryor's quick thought, "and he give it to 'em on my account, pore old feller."

The report brought down by Evers electrified Leadville, used as it to big strikes in the Gulch. Everybody trooped up to the Potato Hole, as the mine had been named by its discoverer, Nevada Charlie.

In the afternoon light, the heavy, wide vein of silver and leaden metals gleamed dully. Sam Wilton, Old Mac, and the rest of the owners stood about, faces red with excitement over the strike which promised them, surely, riches and fame.

"Yuh're rich, folks!" cried Mayor Tabor, congratulating everybody about him. "Good luck, and hurrah for Leadville!"

Next morning, the Rio Kid rode out of Leadville with Horace Tabor, and his trail-mates. He left behind him the people he had helped. They had had, thanks to him, a surprising stroke of good fortune. As joint owners of the new mine they would all be wealthy. And too, thanks to the Rio Kid's mighty guns, they were apparently safe.

Tabor's reports, and advices obtained by Bat Masterson and the Rio Kid, told that George Smothers and Squirrel Hart, with the gunnies who had worked for Bull Olsen, had taken to the tall timber. They showed no signs of coming back to face the deadly music written for them by the flaming Colts of the Rio Kid.

Because of the Rio Kid's swift diagnosis of the trouble in Leadville and his smashing victory, Horace Tabor felt able and safe to leave the town and his many interests there. Unlike Nevada Charlie, Tabor had heirs to his holdings. He had partners and other strings to his fortunes.

To have seized his wealth would have been a complicated procedure, whereas old Charlie had been alone. But the Potato Hole had become the property of Evers, Wilton and their friends. The Maiden's Prayer and Charlie's town lots, however, were being held for some possible future claimant. If not claimed by distant connections in due time they would pass to the state.

"Olsen was boss of them gunslicks, Bat," remarked Pryor to his partner. "Killin' him was a good stroke. It sort of discouraged the others. As did yore bullets, as well."

"I don't reckon Smothers and Hart'll dare come back," Tabor agreed, nodding, as he listened.

The Rio Kid was pleased enough. He had brought the wagon train through and got the folks in it a splendid start, besides crushing their enemies. At the same time, he was carving out new adventures for himself.

As for the average citizen of Leadville, each was intent on his own pursuit of wealth and saw little of what went on behind the curtain. Miners worked their tours, drank up their wages, died or left for other fields. There were those who preyed on the workers. But the common man unmarked by luck in Leadville cared about nothing that did not directly concern himself.

Out of this mad world, lawless save for the impulses of decent leaders such as Tabor, headed the Rio Kid, to the heart of America's gilded, postwar civilization, the capitol at Washington, D.C.

CHAPTER X

Interlude

☐ Everything that was touched by the florid, good-humored Tabor turned to gold—or silver—as the Rio Kid had heard many times during his sojourn in Leadville. The most amazing streak of luck had suddenly hit the man, when middle-aged and a failure, he had grubstaked those two ragged prospectors to whom he had smuggled a bottle of whiskey when he had fixed up their outfit for them.

It read like the most unbelievable fiction tale that they, after consuming the whiskey Tabor had magnanimously given them from his small stock in his little backwoods store in the Gulch, should have become too intoxicated to proceed to the spot toward which they had been heading, had dug where they finished up the bottle, and had struck it rich. From the moment they had cut Tabor in for a third he had made one fortune after another until he had become known as the "Silver King."

Now, worth millions on millions, Tabor was heading for Washington, to splurge among the big fish.

The Rio Kid had left Mireles and Bat Masterson back in Denver. After a brief stop in the town which was to be the future capital of Colorado, Tabor had caught the transcontinental railroad train and at what to them was stunning speed Pryor and his new friend were whisked across the miles.

Bob Pryor, the Rio Kid, had been in Washington, the nation's capital, on previous occasions when he had been an officer in the Union Army during the Civil War. He had known President Lincoln, and U. S. Grant, now occupying the proud office of the nation's chief magistrate, for Grant had been Pryor's former commander-in-chief.

On arriving in Washington, Tabor with his retinue hurried to the biggest and most famous hotel, the Willard, where he engaged the most expensive suite. Then, taking the Rio Kid with him, he started on a shopping tour, throwing money to the four winds in a fashion that made Pryor gasp.

"I want yuh to have the best, Rio Kid," Tabor shouted, slapping him on the back. "I'll pick it out myself."

He insisted on fitting the Rio Kid out in Western clothing of the most flamboyant type. A huge white Stetson cost two hundred dollars. There were great boots with spurs, the finest of riding trousers, and a leather coat of startling hue and texture.

"New guns, too!" Tabor cried, not yet satisfied. "Pearl-handled, and inlaid with virgin gold."

"I'll look like a fool in them duds, Tabor," objected the Rio Kid.

"My bodyguard must have the very ultra-best!" insisted Tabor.

Late that afternoon, Tabor went out on parade in Washington, his "bodyguard" with him. Tabor wore a new black frock coat, fine trousers and boots, and white ruffled shirt. In his stock a huge diamond stickpin scintillated.

The cuffs of his shirt were over-long, to show the inch-square onyx cuff links, set with big diamonds. On his blunt fingers, which until a few years before were used to the pick and dirt, shone many rings, also set with diamonds of prodigious size. He flourished a gold-headed cane that was studded with jewels, and his long, preposterous mustache was newly and stiffly waxed, the ends up beside his shining eyes.

Slightly in the rear and trying to hide his deep amusement at Tabor's antics, came the Rio Kid. The huge white hat with its curved brim shaded his tanned, handsome face. He wore a yellow jacket with a diamond-clasp pin at the throat where a red silk bandanna with yellow spots showed. Yellow doeskin pants were tucked into high, polished boots on the heels of which were clanking spurs.

At his waist rode a cartridge belt, and in the two holsters were large .45 revolvers, their stocks inlaid with real gold and diamond chips. But under his shirt, the Rio Kid carried two Army Colts, plain, tried pistols. For he had no faith in the fancy weapons he had donned at Tabor's insistence.

Even in Washington, used at the time to Gold, Silver and other "Kings," Tabor attracted attention. Citizens turned to stare with dropped chins at the two-man procession, while others snickered openly.

Tabor had introductions to prominent people, congressmen and lobbyists. His money was an open sesame in many quarters. On the night of his arrival he gave a dinner for two hundred guests in the private ballroom at the hotel, and the finest of foods and wines were served.

Tabor basked in the limelight, his voice ringing through the halls. He was slapping senators on the back, and the Rio Kid, in his fancy duds, watched the game, smiling indulgently. For no one could dislike Horace Tabor. The man was open and good of heart. His charities, his helping hand to those who needed it, were well-known.

"It ain't my kind of life, though," mused Pryor. For the moment, he was off to one side, for Tabor was surrounded by others.

The party lasted until dawn. Before it was over, the Rio Kid slipped away and turned in. He never overdrank and the Tabor party was turning into an orgy.

It was not until next evening that the Rio Kid again

79

saw Tabor. The Silver King had slept all day and was breakfasting when most people were ready for supper. Tabor grinned at the Rio Kid across the white-clothed table set in his private suite.

"How'd yuh like the party, Rio Kid?"

"Oh, fine."

"Guess what! Next week we're goin' to meet General —President Grant!"

The Rio Kid started. Grant had been his old commander-in-chief—

"Yuh don't mean to drag me along, do yuh, Tabor?"

"Oh, shucks, don't be bashful. I ain't. Just watch—I'll slap Grant on the back!"

"I'll bet yuh will."

"And"—Tabor lowered his voice slightly—"one of these days *I'll* be President of the United States, Rio Kid!"

"I wish yuh luck."

No one, not the Rio Kid, and certainly not Horace Tabor himself, could foresee that within a few short years his hundreds of millions of dollars would evaporate far more rapidly than they had accumulated, that he would be a pauper, once more digging in the Colorado dirt, an old, broken man. But before that happened one of his lifelong ambitions was to be satisfied. For when Colorado did become a state he was State Senator—for one month, to fill out the unexpired term of the senator who was elevated to the Federal Branch.

"How long," inquired the Rio Kid, "yuh figger on stayin' in Washington this trip, Tabor?"

"Oh, a month, maybe two or three. Might make it all summer if need be. I got to set up my influence, Rio Kid. Colorado has got to be a state, and I've got to see to that."

"Huh! Who wants to be a polertician, Tabor?"

"Me, for one." Tabor lowered his voice again, his eyes bulging. "Tell yuh a secret, Rio Kid. The boys back in Denver are goin' to run me for senator just as soon as ever they can—which is one good reason why Colorado has got to be a state."

That night Tabor threw another big party, hiring a troupe of beautiful dancing girls to entertain his guests. To the Rio Kid it was amusing, a different world from the wild frontier with its violence. And yet, beneath the gilt, beneath the attitudinizing of the power- and wealth-seeking multitudes who swarmed in Washington, the Rio Kid sensed the same predatory scheming, the same life-or-death struggles that went on in the wilderness. But here it was done by lies and words instead of being settled with honest Colts.

"Guarding" Tabor in Washington was a different matter from the job in Leadville. Here the Rio Kid was part of Tabor's political color scheme, an adjunct to call attention to Tabor's person. He was gaped at when he strode, swaggering as Tabor wished, along the main streets of the capital. Urchins followed him, eyes wide, begging to touch the fancy Colts he wore, shouting at him.

There was no danger to Tabor from bullets. The violence here was of a different nature and much more dangerous.

When the great day arrived that Horace Tabor was to be received at the White House, in his resplendent garb, he broke into the reception room where the President awaited him.

This was the focal point of the universe, and the rather stubby man in a rusty-looking black suit, with his bearded chin sunk on his chest and a cigar clenched in the corner of his mouth, was the hub of it all.

U. S. Grant, hero of the Civil War, was in the White House. Every man in Washington sought the President's ear, begging for the power that meant wealth. Grant, honest and sturdy himself, was a great soldier but not a trained politician. He was being fooled, behind his back, by rapacious officials.

"President Grant!" bawled Tabor, running to him with a fat hand outstretched. "This is the greatest pleasure of my life!"

He seized Grant's hand and pumped it, grinning from

ear to ear. And, with the expansive gesture of frontier good-fellowship, he clapped the President on the back.

"I done it!" cried Tabor.

Grant's eyes took in the flamboyant Tabor whose gems glistened in the light from the high windows. The eyes were narrowed, but suddenly they fell upon the Rio Kid, standing there in his full glory, according to Tabor's ideas, and they widened. Grant started in surprise.

The Rio Kid came to attention and saluted, and the President recognized him. He had known Bob Pryor as a fine young captain of cavalry during the war.

"Yuh savvy my bodyguard, Mr. President?" asked Tabor. "Meet the Rio Kid, fastest man on the draw west of the Missouri and a square-shooter."

The Rio Kid had read the amazement and then the amusement which Grant tried to conceal, as the President took him in. The fancy duds and guns gleamed.

"I knowed it'd give Grant a laugh to see me," thought the Rio Kid, pleased with his effect. "I reckon he can do with one, too. He looks mighty tired. Bein' President is worse than fightin' through the Wilderness."

"Captain Pryor," murmured Grant, "this is indeed a surprise."

Bob Pryor grinned, and Grant's taciturn face suddenly broke into a wide smile. One eye winked at the Rio Kid, and he was laughing with his friend Bob Pryor.

"He savvies," mused the Rio Kid.

Grant waved a hand holding his cigar, to invite his guests to be seated.

"Yes, Mr. Tabor," replied Grant, "I know the Rio Kid. We met in the army. Now what can I do for you?"

"I come to pay my respects," Tabor told the President, "and offer my services to the party. We're back of yuh in Colorado, General, back of yuh to the limit."

"Thank you. I hope to see the famous Leadville one of these days—perhaps when you are senator."

Tabor stopped grinning for a moment, gawking at the President.

"What did yuh say, General?"

"Why, I merely mentioned, sir, that you quite likely will one day be senator. I understand you are interested in working for Colorado statehood, a matter which is interesting many at the present moment. I have also heard that you have been selected by general acclaim by your friends back in Denver to stay here in Washington a month or two, to lend your energies toward what the citizens of Colorado so much desire."

Tabor gulped. His eyes were bulging from their sockets.

"I ain't heard about that, yet," he mumbled. "Been out all afternoon. I reckon the wire's at the hotel."

"Washington is going to enjoy your presence, Mr. Tabor, I can see that. Isn't that so, Captain Pryor?"

"Yessir," replied the Rio Kid. "It shore is. And rightly so. Tabor's a square-shooter, General—I mean Mr. President."

"I like General better," murmured Grant, "especially with old friends like you, Captain."

After the interview, Tabor walked on air. The Rio Kid escorted him back to his big suite in the Willard and there Tabor found several wires awaiting him, among them the one from Denver announcing that he had been selected to stay in Washington and work for Colorado's statehood.

Tabor was deeply affected. It was some time before he recovered his brash egoism. Then he opened the other telegrams which had come.

"Look at this one, Rio Kid," he ordered, tossing a wire to Pryor.

The Rio Kid read:

HAVE COMPLETED DEAL ON THE LAST CHANCE AS YOUR LATEST TELEGRAM ODERED. YOU'RE A DANGED FOOL, HORACE. I RESIGN.

FRANK.

"Frank's my Leadville manager. The Last Chance is

83

my best-payin' mine out there. I don't savvy what he means. I better wire him."

Tabor wrote out a communication to Frank White, his Leadville agent. A day later it was answered, not by White, but by a subordinate. It read:

FRANK LEFT TWO DAYS AGO FOR DENVER. LAST CHANCE SOLD TO SYNDICATE AS PER YOUR WIRED INSTRUCTIONS.

"I don't savvy what it's all about," growled Tabor. "I ought to head back to Leadville and pertect my interests, Rio Kid. But I can't leave just yet. I got to stick around here awhile, seein' as I've chose to stay here and work for Colorado. But I got a funny feelin' inside, Bob." Tabor was deeply troubled, as he watched the Rio Kid. "Tell yuh what. I figger you better head for Leadville hotfoot and see what's up."

The Rio Kid resumed his more usual garb and caught the first train west out of Washington. He was glad to see the last of the "civilized" capital in the throes of its Gilded Age.

By the time he arrived in Denver and located Mireles, who was caring for Saber and his own horse at an outlying livery stable, he had been away from Leadville for weeks.

"Where's Bat?" he asked his trailmate as Celestino's lean, dark face lighted on seeing him.

Saber ran over to the fence to nuzzle his master's hand and complain at having been left behind.

"Señor Bat, he go back to Dodge Ceety," explained the Mexican lad. "I am glad to see you, General."

Fate was rolling its perilous dice, life and death. The Rio Kid saddled up and, with his comrade, hit the trail for Leadville.

CHAPTER XI

Death Strikes Hard

☐ In the meantime, after the departure of the Rio Kid, Bat Masterson and Horace Tabor, Evers and his friends had worked from dawn to dusk on their Potato Hole mine.

It looked bigger and bigger as they uncovered the second vein, deep in the ground.

"We need machinery, boys," Sam Wilton announced when they met one evening. "We can get some on credit, I reckon, with our prospects."

Men had been around, making offers on the mine but they had steadfastly refused to sell, preferring to hold on and win the full riches of the lead carbonates and silver ores.

Everybody was vastly excited, and pictured themselves as millionaires. News of the new strike had spread like lightning and all in Leadville had heard of it at once, while the bonanza was exaggerated with each recounting.

Lead and silver were different from gold. They took refining, capital to invest in machinery, time to pay unless a prospector sold out for cash. In the meantime, the miners needed food, clothing, and shelter.

Wilton, Evers and other leaders were delegated to visit

the bankers, and a loan was negotiated on the strength of the vein they had hit. The money was immediately invested in necessary food and other personal needs, and machinery was ordered. It would have to be shipped up through the Royal Gorge of the Arkansas to Leadville by wagon, an arduous, expensive task, and it would be some time before it could arrive.

Evers had been sorry to see the Rio Kid leave. He missed his friend, but the exciting strike and hard work kept him occupied. Besides, there was Dorothy Wilton. He saw her regularly, and the girl smiled on him, but whenever he tried to bring up the subject of marriage, Dorothy would turn him aside.

"Now look, Dorothy," Evers said one evening, managing to find her alone, "Yuh got to talk to me."

"It's a lovely evening," the girl murmured. "Father wants to take a little stroll, so—"

Evers seized her hand, would not let her return to the smoky light of the camp where several crude shacks had been thrown up, made of raw-cut timber from the mountain slopes. One of them belonged to Wilton.

"Yuh got to admit yuh're wrong, Dorothy—I won't let yuh go till yuh do. I mean, about minin'."

"You'll have to hold on a long time," she said coolly, looking straight up into his eager, handsome young face.

"That suits me. I'll hold yuh forever. We've struck it rich. Will yuh marry me now?"

But she only shook her head.

One evening, some days after the Rio Kid had left town, Old Mac slipped away and Evers hurried after his partner in the dark.

As he was hunting for Old Mac, Evers saw a handsome equipage draw up in front of the Giltedge, and a couple of men got down. Evers paused, staring as the lamplight fell on the face of the big man crossing the walk.

"George Smothers!" he gasped. "He's back!"

The small figure that trailed the thief he remembered he also knew.

"Squirrel Hart with him, of course! They got nerve, comin' to Leadville."

But Evers failed to count on the thoughtlessness of the general public. With Tabor gone, the political organization which had kept some control over the mad mining center was falling apart. Nevada Charlie was dead, and Tabor and many of his aides had gone to Denver or to Washington. The rank and file of miners cared for nothing except to get what they could and spend it on wassail and raw whiskey.

"Duggan'll take 'em," figured Evers.

Smothers and Hart disappeared inside the Giltedge. Troubled, Evers resumed his hunt for Old Mac, finally locating him in a saloon on State. He dragged his friend to camp and reported to Wilton that George Smothers was back in Leadville.

"That hombre's like a bad two-bit piece," he declared. "Always turnin' up. But I don't reckon he can harm us now."

Evers was not so sure. Smothers hated them all, and especially Harris Evers, whose exposure of him and whose participation in the gunfight which had cleaned out Bull Olsen and his gang had caused Smothers so much woe. Evers kept a wary eye out for trouble but everything was quiet for a few days.

Then word came that Marty Duggan had been seriously wounded in a night gunfight with unknown assailants.

Rumors also began floating up as to activities in the town. Smothers had money and was splurging. Armed men walked at his side and nobody had tried to call him. And one day when Evers went to Leadville after supplies he saw Turkey Craw with Smothers on Harrison Avenue.

In a saloon, the spots where all the news and gossip flew in such centers on the Frontier, Evers heard more. Tabor had decided to stay for a time in Washington to work for Colorado's statehood, since he was so determined to be U. S. Senator. Tabor's manager, Frank White, had sold Tabor's biggest mine to the Colorado Syndicate and behind that syndicate, it was said, was George Smothers.

"They say," the bartender went on, "that Smothers may be mayor in Tabor's place."

"Smothers—mayor of Leadville?" cried Evers. "Why, he's a dirty thief and killer!"

The barkeeper blinked.

"Better not throw such accusations, hombre," he said in a low voice, "unless yuh're ready to back 'em with bullets. Smothers has got power in Leadville now. They say he was framed by that Rio Kid gunny who was here afore."

"The Rio Kid? He's a straightshooter who only gave Olsen and Smothers what they had comin'! Wish he was here now."

"Well, Smothers has got some valuable mines. The Maiden's Prayer is bein' run by his Syndicate, and the Last Chance is worth ten thousand a week. 'Sides that, he got all Nevada Charlie's town property."

"Dang my hide! How in time did he do that?" Evers was stunned with amazement.

The bartender shrugged. "Dunno. They say a will was found makin' Smothers heir to all Nevada Charlie owned."

Back at the Potato Hole, Evers retailed all this information to Sam Wilton.

"I don't fancy how things are goin', Sam," said Evers. "Smothers has his foot in, all the way. S'pose he takes a notion he'd like the Potato Hole, now we've struck it so rich, along with Nevada Charlie's other holdin's, which I bet he got crooked-like. Smothers has it in for us."

"Shucks, our papers are signed and sealed legal-like. If Smothers bothers us, we can spike his campaign for mayor."

"He ought to be run outa town, Sam. He's gettin' more and more control. Everything's fallin' into his lap.

We ought to come out ag'in him. There's enough of us to cause him plenty trouble."

But in the morning the second vein in the mine suddenly tripled in size. It looked tremendous, and in the excitement Smothers was forgotten.

One evening after supper, Evers made ready to turn in. The camp went to bed early, for they rose at dawn to work the mine.

Around nine p.m. there was a light on in Wilton's little shack. It had a main room, with a lean-to for Dorothy at one end. The floor was dirt, but before cold weather set in it would be necessary for all to build warmer quarters and obtain stoves, for the mountain winters were murderous. Hundreds froze to death in the icy spells.

Most lights were out, but Wilton's stayed on, and Evers, sleeping under a brush shelter Mac and he had thrown up, lay awake watching the single little window square. He was aware that Wilton had gone down into Leadville that afternoon to talk to the bankers about another loan, but thought he had come back.

They had made a few attempts to spike Smothers as the next mayor. Wilton, Evers and others had spoken against Smothers and his gang to miners they knew, and to acquaintances, reviving the known criminality of the man.

Evers saw the cabin door open, and Dorothy stood in the lighted rectangle.

"Harris!" she called softly.

Evers pulled on his boots, jumped up and hurried to her. She looked up into his eyes anxiously.

"Father's awfully late. I'm worried."

"He ain't come back yet?"

"No. He left about three this afternoon and promised to be home for dinner."

"Don't worry," Evers said comfortingly. "Prob'ly he had to oil up them fellers some and took 'em to drink and eat."

Dorothy shook her head. "I don't think so. Will you do something for me, Harris?"

"Yes, anything at all."

"Ride down and find father."

"All right, I'll go right away."

Evers went back to his bivouac and strapped on his gun-belt, for the sake of ordinary precaution. Holdups were as common as dirt after dark in Leadville. Thousands had come to the wild town expecting to get rich quick, but finding not even work so they could buy food, had turned to the road as the only way to exist.

The owners of the Potato Hole had mules which they used to drag scoops from the mine, and Evers saddled one and rode out of camp toward town.

The mule plodded steadily along for half the distance. The brush and pines cast dark shadows on the trail, while above, the stars and a slice of moon gave a faint illumination.

Reaching a curve, the mule suddenly stopped moving and refused to go on, despite Evers' urgings.

He got down and tried to pull the animal forward, but the mule would not budge. Evers cursed the beast and tried to discover what had got into him. The mule had his ears up and was staring at a dark clump of bush to the left.

As Evers, his eyes accustomed to the dimness, followed the mule's point, he saw a couple of dark objects lying on the grass, sticking from the brush. Curious, he went over. They were boots, men's boots, and his heart gave a quick turnover in his chest, for he recognized them.

The boots were filled with flesh and bone, but the body was lifeless, as Evers dragged out the man.

As he had guessed and feared, recognizing the footgear, it was Dorothy's father. Sam Wilton was dead. There was a big bullet-hole in the back of his head and he had evidently been waylaid. His pockets had been turned out, and he had been tossed into the bush.

Harris Evers swore as dizziness hit him. He would have to tell Dorothy, and the enormity of the tragedy hit him hard. He had grown fond of Sam Wilton and had counted him as a good friend.

He didn't know whom he was cursing, who had killed Wilton. It looked like an ordinary highway robbery and plenty such occurred around Leadville.

The mule sniffed, not liking the dead body. He pulled up his head and kicked as Evers seized the reins to keep him from retreating.

"Stand still, curse you!" Evers growled.

The beat of heavy hoofs came to him, approaching from Leadville.

"Sounds like an army!" he muttered.

Stepping around the turn, Evers could see for some distance down the moonlit trail.

Many riders were coming up, toward the camp. There were several out in front, and a large bunch, too many to count at a glance in the dim night.

"Hey, gents!" sang out Evers, thinking them miners returning from a party in Leadville. "This way! Murder!"

They came straight at him, pounding in.

"Who's that?" a man in the lead called.

"My name's Evers. I'm from the Potato Hole Mine, and I've just found my friend Sam Wilton dead in the bush. Robbers must've—"

Evers broke off with a startled curse. He could see the faces under the hats now, and realized the riders were all masked.

As he jumped back, his hand dropping to his pistol, a high-pitched voice shrieked:

"Give it to him! It's that young skunk!"

"Turkey Craw!" Evers thought, as he caught the whining intonation of the voice.

CHAPTER XII

Kill 'Em All!

☐ A rider, the one who had yelled and whom Evers believed to be the thief who had once been a member of their party, threw up a pistol and fired quickly at the moving Evers.

The bullet cut a swathe through the flesh over the miner's left ribs, shocking him, and he felt the spurt of hot blood from the wound. At the same moment he pulled his trigger, and a horse was hit, throwing its rider over into the trail and causing several more to pile up.

Evers ran back, shooting at the masked men as he went. They had stopped for a moment to untangle themselves in the narrow trail turn, and he made a couple of more hits. One of the masked men fell from his saddle.

A fusillade came too late to finish him. He heard the spattering of slugs in dirt and brush and, leaping on the excited mule, swung the beast and kicked its ribs. The mule was stung by a flying piece of shale, and with a snort dashed up the rocky way at amazing speed, toward camp.

The masked gang reformed swiftly and came after him. It was rough going, however, and the mule was able to stay well ahead, keeping his start.

Evers' great natural strength and his youth enabled

him to bear the shock of his wound. He gritted his teeth, sending long shots back at the bunched foe who were coming up the slope after him. The excitement buoyed him. The fact that Turkey Craw was among the gang, that they were masked and on the side trail to the Potato Hole forced him to guess they were actually heading toward camp to raid and kill his friends.

"A thousand to one they waylaid Wilton!" he decided, as he flashed into the home stretch.

"Potato Hole!" he bellowed at the top of his voice. "Everybody out! Grab yore guns! Bandits! Murder!"

Dorothy's light still burned. The girl rushed to her door, and Evers pounded up and threw himself from his saddle.

"Run, Dorothy—run for the bush! Get up in them rocks and hide! It's an attack—I got to fight!"

"Oh, you're wounded, Harris!"

He was covered with blood, teetering on his feet.

"No time—no time. Run! Yuh'll only hold us back. Take the women and kids into the rocks!"

Men were springing to arms at his alarm. Old Mac was up, his gun-belt on, pistol in hand. The Smythe brothers were out, with shotguns and Colts, as were Johnny Burnett, the Hansons, and all the rest of Evers' friends.

"Robbers—they're comin' to kill us!" shouted Evers. "Douse all lights—get yore women and kids back into the rocks!"

He jumped into the Wilton cabin and blew out the single little lamp. Dorothy had obeyed his orders, and was running to help with the children and older folks, while the men gathered with Evers and Burnett, lining up to fight.

"Where's Sam Wilton?" cried Burnett.

"He's dead, boys, killed by them skunks, I believe," gasped Evers. "I found his body below in the bush. Then when they come ridin' up, I reckernized Turkey Craw's voice. In my opinion, Smothers and Hart and Turkey Craw are fetchin' their bunch of gunnies to wipe us out! Smothers has it in for us, anyways."

93

"Burnett, you take command," said Fred Olds.

"Line out then, boys," shouted Johnny Burnett. "Keep space between yuh and take what cover yuh can! Make every shot count!"

Evers' breath was rasping in and out of his lungs. His wound hurt a great deal, but he reloaded his Colt, and crouched down.

"Here they come!" shouted one of the Smythe boys.

The startled miners could see for themselves. A line of masked riders broke over the crest of the rocky slope, and spurred at the camp.

Within two hundred yards, the attackers whooped and opened fire. Bullets tore the night air, striking the shacks, ricocheting from stones. It was heavy fire, and the miners, counting only three dozen effective fighting men, sought to break the charge.

"Fire!" bellowed Burnett.

His men let go with shotguns and Colts, their tearing lead ripping the charging line.

Three of the gunnies went down, crashing from their horses, but the rest came on.

"Back, boys!" Burnett ordered. "Them wings'll swaller us all in a minute!"

Shooting as they ran, the defenders retreated to another building from behind which they sought to hold back the furious attack. Pausing at the Wilton shack, the riders smashed the kerosene lamp, and set fire to the house. It burned quickly, the red flames licking the dried timber and flimsy walls.

Fighting from shack to shack, outnumbered three to one, the stunned riders delayed the gunnies. But the attackers, dismounting, filtered around. Burnett had lost two men and several had been wounded.

"Can't afford it," he muttered.

The women and children had reached the woods and rocks beyond the camp. They were cut off from Leadville by the deep, rocky gulch and wild mountain country, the open way down being blocked by the attackers.

Harris Evers was growing weaker as he fought savagely back, with his friends, at the pressing gunmen. He was certain that Smothers had at last struck them, and meant to kill them all.

In a lull, he communicated this idea to Burnett, who finally agreed he was right.

"We better run our folks back further, in that case," growled the new leader of the miners. "Evers, yuh're wounded, and yuh been fightin' right through. Take half a dozen of the boys and get goin'. We'll hold these jaybos till yuh're clear."

Evers hated to quit the firing line but he knew Burnett was right. Several mules had run up into the rocks from their picket line, and Evers and his men caught them and hurried to locate the women and children.

As he pressed up the steep slope, through rocks and thick brush, the firing reopened with full-throated fury.

A terrible, stentorian voice echoed in the night:

"Kill 'em, men—kill 'em all!"

Up through the tremendous, high-walled Royal Gorge of the Arkansas River rode the Rio Kid, on his return to Leadville. Celestino Mireles, his faithful partner, was with him, as they headed for the mad mining center perched in the Rockies.

Fate had rolled those dice, to send the Rio Kid to Leadville again, all unknowing the tragedy and death that had struck his friends during his absence.

Disquieting rumors were going the rounds in Denver, though. It was said Tabor was slipping, up in Leadville, and that a new boss of the town was in the making. But the Rio Kid had not waited to check what he had heard. He had saddled up and hurried through the passes as soon as he had been given an inkling that trouble might lie ahead.

Nearing Leadville, he could not say what caused it but some innate warning came to him. The old war wound in his side began to itch, as it often did when danger threatened.

His clear eyes alert and ahead, and with Saber's head

down as he strained up the slope, the Rio Kid hit Leadville and Harrison Avenue at its far end.

"She's grown twice as big since we left a few weeks ago, Celestino," he remarked.

The mines were going full-blast in the warm sunshine of the late afternoon. There were hundreds of horses and teams crowded at the hitch-racks and in the corrals of livery stables and open spaces. Those out of work or not, desiring it for other reasons, thronged in the shade outside the saloons and honky-tonks.

Proceeding into the heart of town, the Rio Kid, suddenly pulled up short in the middle of the road.

"Well, dang my hide!" he exclaimed. "Look up there, Celestino!"

The Mexican's dark eyes raised to fix a piece of white canvas stretched from roof-pole to roof-pole over the avenue. In huge black letters it read:

OUR OWN GEORGE SMOTHERS
FOR MAYOR!

"More over zere, General," muttered Mireles, pointing.

The whole town was plastered with signs, demanding that Smothers be elected in Tabor's place, that the latter was to live in Washington, and a new election would be held. There were other candidates, but Smothers evidently had by far the most publicity, and while the Rio Kid and Mireles paused, they saw a couple of armed men in Stetson and leather, tear down another aspirant's signs.

"So that's how he's hoggin' it all," mused Pryor. "This is mighty interestin'. I'm glad I come back. Let's see what Marty Duggan has to say. Smothers! A bad egg always turns up, ain't it so?"

"*Si*—eff zere ees one bad apple, it always comes to han'."

They rode slowly on, weaving in and out of the traffic.

"There's the Giltedge—and hanged if Smothers ain't right out in plain sight!" growled the Rio Kid.

George Smothers, in elegant new clothing and a dark, narrow-brimmed derby hat, stood on the porch of the big saloon on Harrison Avenue, surrounded by friends. The ubiquitous Squirrel Hart hovered close at hand.

Leadville had changed, as rapidly as it was growing. Hopefuls were pouring in from other fields, from the east, north, south and west.

"I'm goin' to speak to Duggan, first," growled the Rio Kid. "He'll tell me what's up."

CHAPTER XIII

Return

□ Pulling up, the Rio Kid dismounted in front of the city marshal's office, in a building near the Giltedge Saloon.

The door was wide open and he stepped inside, expecting to see the rough but honest Duggan. A man was sitting at the desk, with his booted feet up, and he wore the marshal's star—but it wasn't Marty Duggan.

"Turkey Craw!" exclaimed the astounded Rio Kid. "What in thunder are you doin' with—"

The bony horse-thief opened his eyes, staring with disbelief at the Rio Kid. He was as amazed to see Pryor as the scout was to see him. He was not his old tattered self. Instead he was wearing blue trousers, tucked into new boots, a blue shirt with the badge pinned on it, and his sandy hair had been recently trimmed. The weak chin and washed-out gray eyes were the same, however, and they showed his abject fright as he recognized the man he feared most in the world.

"The Rio Kid!" screamed Turkey Craw at the top of his lungs.

Then he pulled his legs in so fast that the chair tipped over backward and he sprawled under the desk.

"He's goin' to kill me—Murder!" shrieked Turkey Craw. "Help—Outlaw—Killer!"

"Shut up, yuh blasted fool," snarled the Rio Kid, kicking him in the slats.

Heavy steps sounded in the back room, and a bunch of men, wearing deputy badges, leaped to the office door from the rear of the building. They had come at Turkey Craw's shrill calls, and they were all armed. Among them the Rio Kid recognized a couple of merrymen who had belonged to Bull Olsen's gang, and they dug for their Colts on sight.

"Kill him!" bawled one. "That's the Rio Kid! He's outlaw here!"

"General—General—pronto, more come!" cried Mireles, sticking his head in the door, as he stood holding the horses.

A pistol exploded from the adjoining room, the slug narrowly missing the Rio Kid and tearing splinters from the doorway. The Rio Kid, seeing half a dozen guns rising to blast him, made a lightning whip of his Colt, the hammer spur back under his trained thumb which, rising, allowed the hammer to fall on the cartridge.

A man in front, one of Smothers' bunch, took Pryor's first bullet in the hip. The crack of bone was as sharp as that of the explosion, and the man's screams as he fell, bleeding, to the floor, rang deafeningly in the office. Turkey Craw, flat on the floor, was begging for mercy, and made no attempt to use the guns he wore.

The Rio Kid, busy with the bunched killers only a few paces across the office, had no time to deal further with the cowardly horse-thief. He was moving back, face to his opponents, alert, swift, bullets from his Colt roaring into them as he fired with terrific speed.

Appalled by his desperate, unerring gun courage they felt the lead of death cutting them, singing close, the smashing fire right in their faces. A couple were hit, and the rest discharged their revolvers too soon, so that they missed the moving Pryor entirely.

He jumped back out of the door. Mireles was already mounted, holding Saber ready. The Rio Kid sprang to the saddle without touching iron, starting along the sidewalk close to the building wall.

"There he goes! It's the Rio Kid!"

Squirrel Hart, on the walk in front of the Giltedge, pointed frantically toward the two riders, urging on a dozen more gunnies who had dashed from the saloon. Smothers was up on the veranda, watching the scene. He was giving orders to the men who obeyed him.

Bullets came after Pryor and Mireles. They swung in their saddles to throw lead back at their enemies. The Rio Kid tried for Smothers and Hart also, but they were well-covered, and Smothers' gunmen were piling up on the fugitives.

"This way, Celestino!" ordered the Rio Kid, cutting down a side alley.

They rode at a mad gallop through to the back street, turned south and tore past the piles of garbage and tin cans which chronically surrounded the buildings of Leadville. The wind was coming in from the smelters, whose stacks belched heavy, grayish-black smoke, fouling the clean mountain air with sulphur dioxide and other unpleasant odors.

The sun was crimson over the peak, Mt. Massive, which cast its tremendous shadow for a long distance.

Saber and the swift, long-limbed gray mustang which the horse-loving, expert Mireles had picked up in Denver, flew out of town.

"We'll head for the Potato Hole!" panted the Rio Kid. "Wilton and Evers'll tell us what the devil's up!" He broke off, as a swift thought hit him. "That is, if they're there."

The various odors were identified by his olfactory senses as he rode. A big saloon gave off the damp, beerish odor common to such establishments. Next came a restaurant, where food was cooking. Then as the Rio Kid inhaled, he caught the warm, sweet odor of a bakery, an odor unmistakable.

The door and windows were open in the afternoon

heat. As he galloped past, for an instant glancing in, he saw a girl standing near the door, her rounded arms white with flour and her hands covered with the dough she was working at a nearby table.

He had but a quick glimpse of her startled face. He thought he recognized her, but wasn't certain.

"Dorothy—no, couldn't be—" was his swift thought.

A bullet ventilated his Stetson, and a howling pack of gunmen, reinforcements who had been started after him by Smothers and Hart, ripped through into the alley, spewing from several openings and shooting wildly after the two riders.

There was no time to waste on anything. The Rio Kid took another side turn and came out on State Street, that squalid street where the poorer miners took their pleasures. He dashed past Dinty's, where he had gunned Olsen, Smothers and the rest that night which seemed so long ago.

Heading for the Potato Hole, and gaining easily on the pursuit, the Rio Kid and Mireles made it in record time up from Leadville. They took the shortcut, avoiding the canyon proper, and went through the bushy, rocky trail up to the site of the camp of their friends.

Hitting the spot where the shacks had been, they saw the burned ruins of the little homes. There were miners around—but they were strangers to the Rio Kid, these bearded, rough fellows now working the claim. Ore was being taken out, crushed, and being made ready to go to the smelter, but among the men handling it there was not a familiar face.

A couple of foremen appeared and swung as they caught the sound of the clicking, pounding hoofs approaching. The Rio Kid recognized those two men all right. They were both friends of George Smothers, followers of the defunct Olsen. The Rio Kid had fought a gun battle with them, and their partners.

"Hey, there's the Rio Kid!" one of them yelled instantly.

"This way, boys—fetch yore guns!" bawled the other. "There's a thousand dollars reward for that skunk of an outlaw!"

Snatching up shotguns, two foremen blazed away at the approaching Pryor. The scattering buckshot was dangerous, covering a wide area as it spread. One tore into the Rio Kid's leather-clad right leg and made a painful flesh wound, and Mireles cursed as another bit his dark-skinned high-boned cheek.

The Rio Kid's Colt snarled back. He downed the two foremen with as many shots, for he was trained, from long years in the Army and on the Frontier, to shooting from a moving horse's back. The pair of killers folded up under their weapons, while a horde of workers, miners hired by the company, taking their bosses' word for it, dug for their pistols.

"Let's get outa here!" ordered Pryor. "Smothers has control and he's lied us into outlaws!"

Before they could suit action to the words, however, shouts rose from the trail along which the Rio Kid and Mireles had just ridden. The gunnies from Leadville were coming after them, urged on by Smothers and Hart. Now, on one side they had the miners, whooping and cursing at the two they believed to be outlaws, and preparing to send a volley at the Rio Kid, and Smothers' gunnies on the other.

Pryor, stunned by his welcome back to Leadville, urged his sure-footed dun over the brink of a rocky slide. Saber dug in his hoofs, and threw back his head, nearly falling, but reached the bottom safely and ran across a rough stretch to the narrow opening of a cut.

Behind him, as he glanced around, the Rio Kid saw that the skillful Mireles, born to a saddle, had negotiated the dangerous drop without crashing. He was coming at the dun's heels, low over his animal's neck, talking soothingly to the gray.

For the time being, due to this move, they were out of sight of the ravening gangs, and the bulge of the hill protected them from bullets. Then the advance guard of the pursuers reached the brink, shooting after them. The Rio Kid tore into the cut, and after him came Mireles. There they again had protection from the rocky walls. Howls of baffled fury came from the throats of their foes, and the lead sent after them shrieked harmlessly into dirt or through the darkening air.

The worst of it was over, as the Rio Kid and his friend made distance, retreating out of Leadville's vicinity. An attempt was made by the pursuers to keep after them, but in more open country, on the back-trail to the Royal Gorge, they could not be overtaken. At last night threw its velvet blanket over them and the scratched, weary men and horses could rest.

Taking stock, by the side of the Arkansas, which mighty river here was only a good jump for a horse, the Rio Kid found he was one hundred per cent aroused.

"Smothers has shore sewed up Leadville while we been away—me with Tabor—Celestino," he growled, squatted on his haunches as he fixed a smoke. "He's made me an outlaw and turned decent folks agin me. But he savvies I'll fight him, hard, and he wants me dead."

The horses had been unsaddled, picketed where they could graze. Pryor washed and bound up the Mexican's flesh wounds, and Celestino did the same for his comrade. They had cold food in their saddle-bags. Making a little fire in the shelter of a rock, coffee was fixed.

"What happen to zee people of the wagons?" Mireles asked, as they rested themselves after their meal.

"Huh! That's what I got to find out. Smothers has jumped their claim, that's plain, and chased 'em to the devil and gone. Duggan's quit as marshal, Tabor's in Washington, and Leadville looks like it was Smothers' plum, cuss him. That was as close a squeak as we could have, this afternoon. Them sidewinders have bought and shot their way in, and they're here to stay."

"What now?"

"Sleep, first. The hosses need a breathin' spell, more'n

we do. Then I'm goin' to check up and if I can I'll cook Smothers' goose for him . . . Say, did yuh see that young lady when we passed the back door of the bakery?"

Celestino shook his dark-haired head. He had taken off his peaked sombrero and the straight black hair beneath it was matted with sweat. In the gloom his eyes shone like twin red coals.

"I am too bus-ee, General. I look only at zose hombres."

"I'll take my oath it was Dorothy Wilton, but what in tarnation would she be doin' there?"

The Rio Kid was unable to explain his self-asked question. He was determined, however, to discover the answers to all the riddles he had come upon.

Sleep was necessary, and while the horses were recuperating, the two rolled in their blankets and quickly drifted off, untroubled by the terrific fight they had gone through.

In the first gray touch of the dawn, with the cool mountain air fragrant with summer's breath, the Rio Kid and Mireles rose. They cleaned up at the stream, watered the horses, and ate breakfast.

It was not yet light, and the mists were still hanging on the mountain meadows, but there was enough illumination to pick the way back to the main road that led to town. Cautiously approaching Leadville, while the day slowly but surely grew, the Rio Kid found most of the mad city still in bed. Only a few early risers were about.

They met none of their enemies, as they rode by back ways to the alley and the bakery where Pryor believed he had seen Dorothy Wilton. Bakers rose early, to get their wares ready for the day's trade, and this was no exception. For this one was up and about.

Now to find the answer to at least one question.

CHAPTER XIV

Hidden Camp

☐ Just as the Rio Kid drew up nearby, the door of the bakery opened and a man in shirtsleeves and a white apron came out. He unlocked a shed across the alley, and began rolling out a barrel of flour.

Pryor handed his reins to Mireles, dismounted, and strolled over.

"Miss Wilton up yet, Mister?" he asked.

The baker paused, looking at him. "Huh?"

"Miss Wilton, the young lady who works here. She's a friend of mine."

"Go on—beat it," the baker growled. "She don't like mashers."

"I'm no masher! Keep a civil tongue in yore head."

The fellow bristled, but seeing the look in Pryor's eye, and the guns at his hip, shrugged and turned away.

"Bob!"

Dorothy Wilton had come to the door and called to him softly.

She wore a white dress, clean and freshly starched, and looked as pretty as a picture. She had a white ribbon around her taffy-hued hair, and her large violet eyes and peach-bloom complexion had never been lovelier.

"Dorothy!" exclaimed the Rio Kid, seizing her outstretched hand. "I'm mighty glad to see yuh. Did yuh recognize me when I flew by last evenin'?"

"Yes. I was afraid they'd catch you and kill you. I'm glad they didn't, Rio Kid." She spoke quietly and steadily.

"I rode in yesterday and right into trouble," he told her. "Smothers has taken over yore mine and the town, far as I can make out."

The girl nodded. She was about the most beautiful girl he had ever seen, thought the Rio Kid.

"I heard about it later," she said. "That is, how you escaped from those fiends."

"Where's yore dad?"

"He was shot and killed one night not long after you left," the girl murmured.

The Rio Kid jumped. Anger flushed him.

"Smothers' bunch done it, I s'pose?"

"I'm not sure. Nobody is. But I think so."

She had recovered from her first grief and had accepted Fate's terrible blow with resigned fortitude.

"And Evers, and all the others?"

"Harris was wounded in the fight that followed. He found Father's body on the trail to camp, and while he was there, masked gunmen came along and fired on him. The rest of us managed to escape in the darkness, though several of our men were killed and wounded."

"Where are they now?"

"Hidden, somewhere in the mountains." She glanced around apprehensively, whispering her information. "I came to Leadville for my Father's funeral. No one bothered me, and I hate living out in the camps, so I found this job. It's nice here, and they treat me well."

"And—Smothers jumped yore claim! The Potato Hole, that Nevada Charlie gave yuh all!"

Dorothy told him everything, freely, succinctly.

"He did," she said. "Smothers hates us. He was afraid of Father and Harris and all of us, because we were against him and trying to make the people here realize how bad a man he is. He's running for mayor and I be-

106

lieve he thought we would spoil his chances if we kept talking. And then, the Potato Hole got bigger and worth more. Smothers took over all Nevada Charlie's other property, and I suppose he wanted our mine, too. He's running the Maiden's Prayer through his Syndicate and they have the Last Chance, which Horace Tabor sold them."

"Tabor's agent and manager here sold it, not Tabor," the Rio Kid said tightly. "I figger fake wires were sent to White. I ain't been able to contact him yet."

"I'm afraid you won't be, either. He was killed in the mountains on his way to Denver. Smothers produced a will in his favor, supposed to have been made out by Nevada Charlie. He also had notes for big sums he said Charlie owed him."

"Forged, like them telegraphed orders to White," growled the Rio Kid. "Smothers'll stop at nothin'. But—well, he's got to get rid of me 'fore he can eat his plums!'"

Dorothy nodded. "I don't doubt all the claims produced by Smothers were forgeries, Bob. He had notes he swore Father had given him, and that was his excuse for taking Potato Hole, after running us into the mountains with his masked gang. Smothers' men are watching all the time and I know that if any of my friends show in Leadville, they'll be instantly killed. Smothers has made you an outlaw, too, with his false charges. He bought over some of the city council and had Turkey Craw made town marshal. Money does it and more and more has rolled in as he takes over."

"Huh!" gritted the Rio Kid. "I'll shore have plenty to say to Mr. Smothers!"

"Be careful—please do!" Dorothy begged. "I'd hate to have you hurt. One man can't do anything much. Smothers has a large gang working for him now, the worst elements in Leadville, outlaws and grafters galore. Everyone's afraid of what will happen if he doesn't do as Smothers orders."

"Yuh can't tell me exactly where to find the boys?"

"No. They've moved camp several times and are far back in the mountains."

"And Evers—is he recoverin' from his wounds?"

"Yes, enough to ride. He came to see me two nights ago, and said he'd be here again."

"When?"

Dorothy hesitated. She eyed the Rio Kid speculatively.

"I'm trying to get him to leave Leadville," she said slowly, "and find a steady job somewhere else. I don't like prospecting."

"Yuh expect him tonight?"

After a time she nodded.

"Perhaps—if he can make it. Sometimes our folks come for provisions during the darkness. But you had better not let yourself be seen in town, Rio Kid. I'm afraid Smothers' men may see you. . . ."

It was well after dark when the Rio Kid slipped back into Leadville, and reached the stable behind the bakery where Dorothy Wilton worked. A faint light shone in the rear window.

Leaving Mireles to guard the two horses in the shadows, the Rio Kid took up his post where he could watch the bakery exit on the alley.

About 9 p.m. a rider came slowly along the narrow way and paused. He dismounted, shoulders hunched, face indistinguishable in the night. Going to the back door of the bakery, he rapped three times, quickly. The door opened and Dorothy looked out.

With the panel of light, the Rio Kid was able to recognize young Harris Evers' tall figure, and heard the low greeting that Evers gave to the girl.

Pryor stepped out softly.

"Evers!" he said.

Harris jumped around, hand dropping to the gun he had strapped about his cloak.

"It's the Rio Kid," Pryor told him. "Don't shoot."

"Jiminy!" gasped Evers, a broad smile breaking over his face. "Yuh shore startled me, Rio Kid! I'm mighty glad yuh're back!"

Pryor pushed him inside the room where Dorothy was waiting for Evers. The Rio Kid shut the door and faced his friend.

"I got in yesterday, Evers. Was shot up on Harrison Avenue by Smothers' bully boys. A lot's happened since I left."

"It shore has!" growled Evers.

He looked a bit pale under his coat of tan but he had nearly recovered from the injuries sustained in the night fracas when Wilton had been killed and the rightful owners of the Potato Hole chased off by force of arms.

"I want yuh to take me to yore mountain camp," the Rio Kid said.

"That's just what we been waitin' for," Evers declared. "Hoped yuh'd come back, Rio Kid. We made some complaints to the law in Leadville but Smothers has sewed everything up, and 'course we just wasted our breath. But we're watchin' our chance. Smothers is gettin' stronger all the time, though. We're low on provisions. Some of the boys come in tonight, to buy what we could afford."

"*Bueno*. I'll ride back with yuh."

An hour later, after Evers had visited with Dorothy, the Rio Kid and Mireles rode the dark mountain trail from Leadville with four men of the hidden camp. Johnny Burnett, the new leader, was with them, and Fred Olds, tough and wiry, serious of mien; Phil Hanson and Evers. They had purchased some bags of flour, tobacco, coffee and a side of bacon with their slim diminishing funds.

"We ain't found any justice in Leadville," Burnett informed the Rio Kid, as they left the lights of the city behind and plunged into the dark pine forest. "They say Smothers has the legal end tied up, with forged deeds and so on. And then he has the men to do anything he orders. We were lucky to save our hides, and nobody in these parts cares much what happens to anybody else. They're too busy tryin' to make their fortunes in the mines."

That, the Rio Kid knew, was true of all mushroom

mining settlements. There was no established law and order, and each man was an individual bent on his own selfish pursuits, intent only on grasping the wealth underfoot. Those who were weak or unlucky fell and were forgotten.

They rode over rough country, into and through deep canyons and across wooded, rocky slopes. It was slow going, and there was little light to ride by.

It was near dawn when they turned off a high ridge, descended at an angle down a sliding mountainside, and dropped to the level of a small, swift torrent, a feeder of the Arkansas.

Following the little brook, tremendous boulders formed an almost continuous giant fence, looming over the narrow trail. At a gloomy turn they were challenged, with the clicking of a cocking rifle.

"All right, boys," sang out Burnett. "We're back!"

Drew Hanson, bearded of face, in cap and dungarees, appeared from behind a rock to greet them. He was Phil's brother, and had been on sentry duty. Another man, a stocky, middle-aged fellow named Vern Brown, was on the other side of the way.

They proceeded, and suddenly the canyon walls widened out on the right into a grassy, sheltered little park. Here, in the rocks, were spread tarpaulins and equipment. It was the hidden camp of the fugitives from Leadville.

The tired riders turned in for what was left of the night.

Refreshed after a sleep in the hidden camp and a wash in the cool waters of the mountain brook, the Rio Kid sought a bite to eat, as the people greeted him with joy and visible relief. He felt they had been looking forward to his return, that they counted entirely on him to lead them out of their trouble.

The sun was up, entering the park to warm the bodies of the luckless fugitives. The women and children were there, and a few pack animals which had carried what they had been able to snatch up. They had also obtained

110

further supplies by secret runs to Leadville in the night. Several wounded men were still laid up. Game could be found in the peaks, although food was short and was rationed.

The Rio Kid, sensing their reliance on himself, braced himself, his clever brain seeking an idea. Smothers was waxing ever stronger, and more firmly established in Leadville with every passing day, while the people he had robbed were growing weaker and could not augment their forces.

"I'll have to hit fast and hard," he muttered.

After breakfast a conference of leaders was called, and the Rio Kid, squatted on his haunches, a cigarette in his fingers, spoke to them, to Burnett, Evers and the rest.

"Boys, it's plain yuh can't stick here forever! Smothers is diggin' in, and we got to rout him out, one way or another, 'fore he's too deep for us."

"We can muster 'bout twenty-five or thirty fightin' men, in a pinch," Johnny Burnett growled, watching the Rio Kid's keen features. "From what I understand, Smothers has a lot more."

The Rio Kid nodded. "True enough, Burnett. But most of 'em are paid gunnies—and that's our best bet. It means they ain't goin' to risk their hides too far, in a scrap. I savvy that sort. They'll fight hot and cruel when winnin' but let 'em take it on the short end and they'll wither up and fade away."

"That's the way to talk!" cried Harris Evers. "Let's go after 'em and have it over with."

"Wait, now," ordered the Rio Kid. "I got a better idea."

He was playing for big stakes, the lives and fortunes of his friends against the evil machinations of the powerful George Smothers, and he threw his own existence in with theirs as he told them his plan.

The struggle for control of Leadville's millions, with the evil Smothers on one side, and the Rio Kid, representing Tabor and the decent element on the other, was fast approaching its furious peak.

CHAPTER XV

The Avengers

☐ Smothers, opulently dressed, with jewels flashing from his hands, sat in the private room of the big Gilt-edge, Tabor's former headquarters.

Men were about him, trusted lieutenants, among them Squirrel Hart and Turkey Craw, his bought law officer. There also were shady politicos who had been only awaiting Horace Tabor's departure before seeking control of Leadville, with its lucrative vice establishments and startling wealth.

Smothers' thick black hair shone with oil, and his beard, shaping his strong jaw, was freshly clipped. His keen black eyes were fixed on a politician with whom he was discussing the division of spoils from a crooked enterprise.

Squirrel Hart, his wiry form encased in a new blue suit, his gray eyes intent, was close to his master, whispering now and then in Smothers' ear. Armed guards were in the corridor, and at the entries, for Smothers took few chances. The windows, too, were covered by alert men.

Smothers had wedged in by promising everyone everything that was asked, aware that once he had consolidated he could break his word without fearing reprisals.

He would by that time have power to smash any opposition and his strong-arm gunmen gang was already formed and ready for action.

Forged documents had given him control of several other lucrative properties than those he had taken from Tabor and from Nevada Charlie's estate. Money with which to pay his fighters has been hard to get at first though. He had been using his capital, brought from the East. But now graft and income from crooked games ranging from cheating gambling devices to plain highway robbery plus the ore taken from the Last Chance, the Maiden's Prayer and the Potato Hole, were pouring cash into his coffers.

In the first flush of his power, Smothers found the snowball rapidly growing in size, and moving with gathering speed.

Tabor's and the Rio Kid's departure, the murder of Nevada Charlie, the forceful jumping of the Nevada Charlie claims, and other circumstances, had been seized upon by Smothers with instant and shrewd judgment. He was chopping away at other of Tabor's holdings, with criminal temerity.

Having taken care of any contingency he could foresee, such as the Rio Kid's return to Leadville, Smothers was not worried over the street fight in which Bob Pryor had so narrowly missed being shot down or arrested. According to the local law, the Rio Kid was now outlaw and with all his friends, was subject to death on sight. Smothers had made sure of that, with his lying charges.

A week had passed since that sudden, boiling gun battle at Turkey Craw's office, and nothing had been heard of the Rio Kid, though a reward was standing for his capture.

It was about ten o'clock as Smothers and his men now sat in the private room of the Giltedge. The evening was warming up as the saloons, filled with half-intoxicated miners, and those who preyed on them, roared at full-blast.

Some quick, heavy steps sounded in the corridor leading from the main part of the Giltedge. The tramping boots shook the flooring, the noise carrying over the squeak of music and the hum of voices up front.

"Hey, what's up, Hal?" an armed gunman at the doorway said.

"Lemme see the boss!" a plug-ugly panted, dashing up.

Hal Burns was a thick-bodied, powerful fellow from Texas. He had been a cowboy for a time, and had turned rustler, had killed a range detective and fled. In his apparel, though, he was still a man of the range, for he wore leather pants and jacket, a sweeping cowboy Stetson, a reversed red scarf and—most important to his calling—a pair of big black Colts whose smooth handles showed how much they were used.

He needed a shave, for his face bristled with a black stubble. His nose was swollen from constant drinking, and his eyes were bloodshot. Now those eyes were frightened though, as he stepped into the room, his chest heaving from his run.

"Say, Boss! Two of the boys just been found in the side street, shot to death and branded!"

"Branded!" snarled Smothers.

"Yessir, branded," insisted Burns.

"Who are they?" inquired Squirrel Hart.

"Harry Fleet and Lew Roberts."

"Two of Olsen's favorites," murmured Hart.

There was a commotion at the back door, and two bodies were carried into the rear of the saloon. Smothers, Hart and all the other men crowded around to stare down at the corpses.

Fleet and Roberts had been among the lot-jumpers who had formerly been led by Bull Olsen, deceased now thanks to the Rio Kid. They had been cruel, blustering killers, but their guns were silenced forever. In fact, the guns had been taken by whoever had killed the men, along with the double cartridge belts which held ammunition.

The death of the two gunnies did not affect Smothers. He felt not the slightest twinge of pity. He could get

114

plenty more where these came from, in the riff-raff of Leadville.

However, he was somewhat worried about one thing. On the forehead of each dead man an "A" had been burned in the flesh by the touch of a hot knife-point. It was about three inches in height and perhaps two wide at the base, and plain in the center of the brow.

Squirrel Hart's quick eye noted something white sticking from the shirt on Harry Fleet's body. He pushed closer, stooped, and drew forth a folded sheet of paper, which he read, then handed to George Smothers.

Smothers read it aloud, before thinking of its possible effect:

THIS IS THE MARK OF THE AVENGERS!
YOU WILL SEE IT AGAIN, ALL WHO DE-
SERVE WILL FEEL IT, AS WELL

"The Avengers!" Hal Burns exclaimed. "That's what the 'A' stands for, then. I never heard tell of 'em. Did any of you boys?"

"Not me," growled a big gunny, shaking his head. His eyes were round as he stared at the brand on the foreheads of the dead.

Smothers and Hart quickly realized how stupid, and only too often superstitious gunnies would take such a matter. He sought to play it down.

"Just some fool playin' tricks," he growled, crumpling up the note and stuffing it in his pocket. "Marshal Craw'll soon settle their hash. All right, boys, outside. Drinks are on me this round. Help yourselves."

"I need one, I reckon," muttered Hal Burns.

Smothers, Hart and the inner circle retired into the sanctum.

"What do you make of it, Squirrel?" demanded Smothers.

Hart shrugged his slight shoulders. His face, if that were possible, was a shade redder than usual.

"I ain't shore, Boss. But—I got a hunch I don't fancy this game."

"Two men are nothin'," Smothers snapped. "Brace up."

Squirrel Hart frowned at the man he followed.

"I figger we'll hear more from these Avenger hombres, Boss. We'll see how far it goes."

"Do you suppose—" began Smothers.

Hart nodded. "I had the same idee myself. If the Rio Kid's in it, we'll have to nip it fast. A thing like this'll spread like wildfire."

"Offer another thousand for the Rio Kid's hide. Curse him, if he's thought this up to devil me, I'll tear him to pieces! Tabor sent him back here, I'll bet my neck. But he can't beat us."

Smothers' fist was clenched, his teeth gritted in his vain fury, while his dark eyes snapped and slitted. . . .

At daybreak, Smothers was awakened by Hal Burns.

"Look here, Boss—they just picked up Kansas City Pete in the gutter. He's got one of them 'A' brands on his forehead!"

"Curse you, I've got to sleep!" snarled Smothers. "Get out of here and keep your trap shut. I'll see you tonight."

But, returning to his elegant bed in the suite of Leadville's best hotel, sleep would not again come to his weary lids. He tossed, almost dozing off, only to start awake. Nightmare visions startled him alert—now a great brown "A" on a skeleton's brow, or other phantasia conjured up in his excited brain.

He got up early, and consumed half a bottle of whiskey. It braced him, and a hot meal helped further.

Walking over to the Giltedge, where he had his office in that big back room, Smothers found Squarrel Hart already there. The little man's eyes showed that he, too, had had trouble sleeping.

"Well?" asked Hart.

Smothers was in a vile humor.

"The more I think of it, the surer I am that the Rio Kid's in on this Avenger business," he snarled.

116

"What good does that do us? Who's ridin' with him?"

"He must have connected with those Potato Hole fools," snapped Smothers.

Squirrel Hart nodded. "That's what I figgered, too. But we ain't been able to locate 'em."

Smothers was standing by the table. He turned, hearing a sound in the corridor.

"Who's that?" he demanded. "Where are all the boys? Where's my bodyguard?"

"I'll see." Squirrel Hart slid swiftly to the door, and glanced into the long hall. "It's just the Mex boy sweepin' up," he announced. "Here comes Burns, now."

Hal Burns came, unsteadily, to the office door. His greeting was thick, sullen. He had already been drinking and there were deep lines in his ugly face. As he passed the cleaner, he booted the Mexican so hard that the lad fell on his face. Two of Burns' gunnies, coming along behind him, laughed, and kicked at the ragged, bare-headed young fellow who cowered in fear against the wall, shrilly begging mercy in Spanish.

He clutched his broom and pan to his bosom with bony hands. His feet were bare, his overalls and old shirt torn. Dirt stained his dark face and his black hair was bound with a ribbon.

He was a typical Mexican of the peon type, in act and dress. There were thousands like him hanging around the camps of the Southwest, working as saloon boys who emptied cuspidors and swept up after the nights of wassail, or ran errands for important citizens. Few people bothered to glance twice at one of them.

"Come in here!" Smothers bawled to his men, and they ceased deviling the Mexican and hurried to the office.

"Now look here, Burns," began Smothers, "I want you to organize the men better, savvy? You're to form a patrol ready to ride at an instant's notice. Post guards at every important street intersection and have 'em signal the moment they see anything suspicious."

"Yuh mean this is agin them Avenger hombres?" inquired Hal Burns.

117

"Yes, just what it is. Shoot to kill! If you down a couple of innocent citizens by mistake, I'll cover you, but smash this up, and pronto."

"*Bueno!*" cried Burns. "Action—that's what I like."

He hustled away to marshal his gunnies.

As the day passed quietly, with no alarms, Smothers began to get hold of himself again. He had a nap in the late afternoon, and after supper and a drink he felt better. He retired to the Giltedge for the evening, with Squirrel Hart at his side.

It was close to midnight when a big gunman known as "Tex" ran through the saloon to the parlor.

"Hey, Boss! They got Hal! Right at State Street and Cross!"

Smothers leaped to his feet with a curse of fury. His eyes snapped and he swore in a dither of baffled rage.

"Where is he?"

"They're fetchin' him in," Tex quavered, backing off before the intense emotion of the boss.

"The fools—they're carryin' him right through the front!" cried Squirrel Hart.

Hal Burns' crumpled form, with a bullet-hole between the left eye and the hairline, was toted up by two members of his patrol. The freshly branded "A" of the Avengers was plain on his brow.

"Where in thunderation is everybody?" shouted Smothers. "Why didn't they stop it?"

"The patrol's tryin' to find them there Avengers now, Boss," Tex informed. "They seen three masked and cloaked hombres down Hal, right under their noses. They wasn't more'n fifty yards away! They're chasin' 'em."

"Only three men! Recognize any of 'em? Was the Rio Kid with 'em?" Smothers spoke eagerly.

Tex shrugged. "They got their faces blacked and keep their bandannas up, Boss. Black *ponchos* or cloaks hide their figgers. I glimpsed 'em myself."

"Maybe the patrol will take 'em," Smothers muttered.

He signaled the half dozen heavily armed gunmen who were on duty as his guard, and strode out to the street.

"Curse it all!" he said to Squirrel Hart. "The whole town'll know of these Avengers now!"

"They do, anyways, Boss," replied Hart. "Everybody's talkin' about it. It spread like wildfire, all right."

CHAPTER XVI

The Human Chain

☐ Furious at the turn of events, Smothers hurried to Cross Street and thence to State, where Hal Burns had died. A narrow, dark passage showed how it had been possible for the three Avengers to creep up on the gunny lieutenant and down him, then escape. No doubt they had had their horses in the alley and ready to get away by rear routes.

In the distance, toward the wild mountains, gunshots sounded, dimly, over Leadville's noise of revelry. But the thoughtless city roared on, oblivious to death and violence.

After half an hour the patrol, made up of fifty picked men, came riding back to the Giltedge. The armed gunnies, labeled with tin badges marked

DEPUTY

dismounted and came into the bar.

Several of them were bleeding from bullet nicks. And outside, three wounded men, groaning and swearing, were being helped into a house, to await a doctor's ministrations.

The leader who had entered the saloon after downing

a couple of quick ones, went with Tex to report to George Smothers.

"Well?" demanded Smothers.

"Well," growled the gunny, "we follered 'em a-sky-hootin' outa town, Boss. Thought we had 'em, 'cause they was just ahaid, but as the trail narrowed down at the turn, we was hit by twenty rifles from both sides and riddled. The ambushers killed four of our fellers and wounded a bunch, more or less serious."

"Tex!" Smothers said, eyes snapping. "I'm goin' to appoint you fightin' chief in Hal's place. You'll get a hundred more a month and bonuses."

"Thanks a-mighty, Boss," Tex replied. "Only trouble is, I ain't much account commandin' men. I'd ruther fight. So if it's all the same to yuh, appoint Popeyes here."

"Popeyes," the big gunny who had led the patrol after the Avengers, blinked.

"It's a honor," he said at last. "Reckon I'll take a stab at it."

Marshal Turkey Craw, his Adam's apple leaping up and down in his scrawny throat, appeared at the doorway.

"Yuh—yuh send for me, Chief?" he chattered.

"Yes, curse you," cried Smothers. "You're marshal of this town. I want these Avengers wiped out, and pronto. Deputize every man in Popeyes' bunch, and stand by to take instant action."

"Yuh mean—agin the Avengers?"

"That's right. We're going to hang every one we don't shoot down."

Turkey Craw gulped. He was not a brave man at any time and now he was actually trembling. He came into the room, and moved close to Smothers, who waved Tex and Popeyes away.

"Boss, I think the Rio Kid's doin' this," Turkey quavered. "I want to quit the job. I ain't suited to it."

He unpinned his badge and laid it on the table. Smothers jumped up, seized him by the throat and bent

121

him back on the edge of the table. He throttled Turkey Craw, getting a little satisfaction out of this violence.

At last he let go, and Turkey Craw sank whimpering to the floor.

"Get up, curse you! You can't quit now. Pin on that badge and go to your office."

It was an hour later that the Rio Kid, standing beside Saber, holding the dun's reins in hand, was peering down through the chaparral fringing the mountainside at roaring Leadville. He could faintly catch the hum of the wicked town as miners, as usual, whooped it up in the dives.

Some quarter of a mile back, resting and waiting for him, was his picked crew of a score, under the command of Harris Evers. Johnny Burnett, Evers and the Rio Kid had been the three who had been in town and finished off Hal Burns that evening. Then they had led the patrol into a neatly prepared ambush.

Tex's men had not stood for long. After a couple of quick volleys they had turned and galloped in ignominious retreat back to Leadville.

The sound now of a swiftly approaching horse made the Rio Kid doubly alert. He was ready for whoever might appear, but he was waiting for some special person, and the rider who dashed along the trail, clinging low over his horse's long mane, was the man.

"Celestino!" the Rio Kid called softly.

"General! *Si!*"

The Mexican youth slid his mustang to a halt and threw himself to the ground.

"How'd it go?" asked Pryor.

"Splendeed, General!" panted Celestino.

The shaft of the moon's rays touched him. He wore ragged clothing and his head was bare, his hair bound by a ribbon. In this radical change of clothing, and the other factors of psychology which the Rio Kid had skilfully used, Mireles had changed from the velvet clad, sombreroed keen fighting partner who rode with the

122

Rio Kid, to a hunched, indistinguishable peon who swept out the Giltedge Saloon.

The Rio Kid had sent his willing friend straight to the heart of the enemy quarters. Celestino had bribed the Mexican who had had the job to quit, and had presented himself a short time later, getting the little desired position as cleaner.

Already Celestino had brought valuable information to the Rio Kid, concerning Smothers' patrol and street guards. And, too, Bob Pryor wanted to identify every member of the great gang infesting Leadville, for the Avengers' attention.

The Avengers had been the Rio Kid's idea. Trying it out, Mireles had reported how well, even beyond expectations, it was working.

"They are loco, like cheecken weeth head cut off," Mireles told his friend. "Turkey Craw try to queet, I hear heem now, before I lef'. Tex refuse' ze job of *vaquero* chief. But a stupeed one name' Popeyes tak' eet. Zey weel covaire every in-trail now, on ze outskirt' of town, at dark tomorrow, General."

"*Bueno*. We're headin' back to camp for a rest and feed now. You be careful, savvy? Don't take any chances yuh don't have to, and meet me here three nights from now, soon as possible after dark."

"Ze only one I fear may savvy me ees Turkey Craw," Mireles said. "But he ees so frighten', he can see nozzing."

"Keep yore face turned away if yuh meet him, and yore hoss ready to make a run for it if yuh have to. I'll see yuh in three days. *Adios*."

"*Adios*, my General."

The Mexican mounted and turned back to Leadville, where he was spying on Smothers for the Rio Kid. Bob Pryor, on Saber, rode to where he had left Evers and the rest of the Avengers. They had their faces blacked where the masks did not cover them and some sort of flowing garment to hide the outlines of their bodies.

"C'mon, gents," ordered the Rio Kid. "We're headin' in for a furlough."

The Avengers were worn out, their horses ragged. They had been lurking in the brush of the mountain gorges for several days, eating cold food, getting none too much sleep. Swinging back for the hidden camp in the hills, the Rio Kid led the way, and they rode all through the dark hours. . . .

Three days later the Rio Kid led his Avengers back to the outskirts of lawless Leadville on time. Faces blacked, cloaks on again, and guns and knives ready for action, they concealed themselves in a wooded ravine while the lithe Pryor went to connect with his town spy, Celestino Mireles.

Over the city, shadowed by Mt. Massive, the immense peak on whose flanks it was set, hung a roseate haze that colored the low-flying clouds. Its wolfish howl penetrated the miles to the Rio Kid's position as he waited for Celestino to come. It was about nine p.m.

For an hour, he hung around, always alert. Then he caught the sound of an approaching horse. It was Mireles, and the Mexican reported to him what Smothers was up to.

"Zey are mucho worry, General. Ten queet and leave Leadveele. Si. Othairs are wait'. Zey covaire ze trails. Zis one ees guard' by three of Smothers' hombres a half mile back. Smothers has sent out a dozen scouts to hunt ze camp where you hide."

"He has, huh! He's clever, at that. H'm. There's a good chance one of 'em may smell us out, if he's really trained at trailin'. I'll have to watch sharp for 'em."

He turned this information over in his mind.

"Where'd yuh say the sentry post is on this back trail tonight?" he inquired after a time.

"You savvy ze beeg fleent rock where she sweeng to south beyond ze brook? Zey hide zere. Three. Now, today, ze gunnies zey feel safer. Nozzing happen for three nights, and zey talk loud how zey hav' scare ze Avengers."

"Off guard—that's fine. I reckoned they would lose their edge after a few quiet nights. Yuh worked around that guard post just now?"

"*Si*. I savvy where zey were."

"All right. Go on back, and listen sharp. I'm goin' to force Smothers' hand. Those folks can't stick up there in the hills forever. It's make or break for 'em."

"How you hope to beat Smothers?" asked Celestino curiously. "He has so man-ee gunnies?"

"I'll tell yuh, soon as I work it all out. In the meantime, stick close to Smothers and keep yore ears open."

The Mexican pressed his friend's hand and slipped away, a wraith in the night. The Rio Kid faded off, picked up Saber, and joined his band of Avengers, under Harris Evers.

They headed for Leadville. It was an easy matter for the Rio Kid and half a dozen picked men to work up around the big flint rock which guarded the approach to Leadville. Afoot—and they had taken off their boots and substituted leather moccasins—the Rio Kid and his six men crept in close to the trio of Smothers' gunnies watching the trail for him.

Three nights with no incident had made them self-confident, and even careless. One was smoking a cigarette, the smoke drifting in the crisp mountain air to the Rio Kid's flared nostrils. The red glow as the man drew on it was plainly visible for yards, and the Rio Kid, creeping in inch by inch, drew up within ten paces without any sound loud enough to startle the three.

Pressed flat to the damp ground for a minute, he lay listening and watching his prey. The smoking man inhaled again, and the glow lit his evil, bearded face. He was one of the deceased Bull Olsen's lot-jumpers, and the Rio Kid knew him as a member of Smothers' gang.

The two were of the same stamp. They were heavily armed, carrying Colts and shotguns, the latter leaning near at hand against a big rock. Their horses were picketed some distance away, in the chaparral.

Evers just behind the Rio Kid touched the leader's

ankle, asking for a signal. The Rio Kid twitched his leg slightly forward, and Evers relayed the signal back to the other black-faced Avengers. Then began the last slow stalk, every inch carefully calculated. They were no more than five paces away when the gunman who had been smoking gave a low cough and threw down his cigarette with a curse, stamping it into the earth.

"This is a no-good job, sittin' out here in the dark," he growled. "Pass the bottle, Dirky."

There was a slight clink of glass, and the Rio Kid could see the flask tipped up, hear the gurgle. The wind rustled the branches, while night insects and tree frogs kept up a continuous piping. Leadville's hum, too, helped drown out the faint noises made by the Rio Kid and his friends as they closed in.

Evers touched the starkly silent Pryor's toes. The Rio Kid wiggled them in his supple moccasins, three times, the signal to get ready to jump. Evers sent the signal back on the human chain.

CHAPTER XVII

The Spy

☐ Ready, and in position, it was the Rio Kid who leaped first, but Evers, Burnett and the others were up an instant later.

"Reach!" the Rio Kid snarled.

The startled gunnies dug for guns, but the Rio Kid's Colt muzzle rammed into a man's ribs and the report was muffled by cloth and flesh. The fellow who had been smoking, the lot-jumper, folded up, dead.

Evers struck a breath afterward, his knife piercing "Dirky's" heart. Two other Avengers fired into the third gunny. None of Smothers' killers managed to get a gun into action, though the third man's gun was rising when he was hit.

It was grim work. As soon as the trio was despatched, the Rio Kid flitted up to the trail to check on whether any patrols might be close enough to have heard the racket. The Avengers swiftly carried out his previous orders.

After a few minutes, the Rio Kid caught the thud of hoofs on the trail, coming from Leadville. He hurried back, and pulled his picked band into the chaparral, where they hid above the flint rock.

A large band of Smothers' gunnies, led by Popeyes, the

new strong-arm chief who had taken the place of Hal Burns after the Avengers had finished with Smothers' bodyguard, rode swiftly up to the flint rock.

"Hey, Dirky!" Popeyes called.

There was no response and the Avengers could hear explosive cursing, and brush crackling as the gunnies cast about, hunting sign. Then Popeyes gave another command, and the whole bunch pushed on, away from Leadville.

"C'mon," ordered the Rio Kid.

His men had fastened the three corpses on the gunnies' own horses which they had picked up immediately after the successful attack.

Hitting the trail recently traveled by Popeyes, they reached Leadville without further trouble. On the outskirts, a knife point was quickly heated and the "A" brand placed on the victims. Sticks tied to the cantle of the saddles propped the dead gunnies up enough so that the Avengers' mark could be seen.

Leading the three horses to Harrison Avenue's terminus where it turned into the mountain trail, the Rio Kid started the mustangs downtown, the dead killers aboard.

Pulling back, they watched as the horses galloped and slowed to a trot, right in the center of town. Men saw the macabre sight, shouted and whooped, and a crowd surrounded the animals as their reins were snatched and held.

"The Avengers!" bawled a man with an especially raucous voice.

"I'd like to snake that Popeyes hombre tonight," murmured Pryor, Chief of the Avengers. "But I figger they'll be as stirred as a beehive after this."

Circling around, they avoided Popeyes' main patrol as it returned to Leadville on the double, hearing the uproar that greeted the arrival of Smothers' three sentries. The Rio Kid took his men to a secret ravine where, under alert guard, they spent the rest of the night and the following daylight hours resting up.

The next night the Rio Kid, feeling carefully for the

enemy, found that, as he had figured, Smothers' men were again alert. He chose Evers and two other Avengers and leading their horses, they worked across rough, rocky stretches without approaching the trails until they were able to enter the main part of the city.

Hidden in the blackness of a stable in the alley running parallel to Cross Street, connecting Harrison and State, the Rio Kid patiently waited for a chance. He saw Popeyes several times as the big, black-browed gunny chief went up or down the street, surrounded by a dozen of his fighters.

It was after midnight before Popeyes made a slight error. He had a lady love who lived in a house on State Street so, snatching an hour off duty, he hurried along Cross Street at full-tilt, alone.

The boardwalk was brightly lighted and there were hundreds of citizens and of his own friends within call. Popeyes felt altogether safe and had his mind on seeing his friend.

The Rio Kid hit him from the side like a launched torpedo. The Army Colt's barrel clonked hard on Popeyes' temple and the tall gunman folded up. Evers caught him as he fell, and they whisked him into the alley.

Five minutes later Evers, who was on guard at the street end of the alley, tiptoed back.

"Rio Kid, here comes Turkey Craw and one of Smothers' hombres!" he whispered.

Pryor had put the finishing touches on Popeyes, who was dead.

"Fetch him up here, boys," he whispered.

Crouched by the corner of the brick wall next the sidewalk, he could see the bony Turkey Craw ambling along, eyes nervously shifting from side to side. He was talking with Tex, the stock gunman who had refused the honor of chief of killers for Smothers.

"Shucks, I reckon the boys'll make a sieve outa this Rio Kid skunk and all his pards," Tex was growling, as they approached.

"Yuh don't savvy that Rio Kid like I do, Tex," Turkey Craw quavered. "He's all tarnation on wheels! He's got it in for me, too. I'm goin' to saddle a hoss one of these nights and light out, that's a fact. Smothers is too rough and asks too much of a man."

Tex, alongside the sniveling Turkey Craw, was a courageous man, though it was fear and native caution which had prompted him to reject Smothers' offer. Turkey Craw's abject cowardice disgusted him, and he spat into the gutter.

"Be a man, Turkey. What the heck, yuh can only die onct. I'll skin that Rio Kid and use his hide for a mat—"

"Lo-ook!"

Turkey Craw stopped, rooted in his tracks by horror and fright. His trembling hand tried to rise, to point at the narrow, dark gap into the sidewalk. Tex, following his line of vision, turned his eyes just as the Rio Kid let Popeyes fall slowly out across the walk.

"Popeyes!"

"Dead!" chattered Turkey Craw, trying to turn and run.

The startled pair saw their crony hit the sidewalk, roll over. And on his forehead showed the mark of the Avengers.

There were miners up the street and down the street. But for some yards the sidewalk was empty, and the Rio Kid stepped out into view. Turkey Craw recognized him and his eyes nearly popped from their sockets. He gave a shriek and fell to his knees, praying for mercy.

But Tex was made of sterner stuff. The gunman swore and ripped out a Colt, making a remarkably fast draw. The Rio Kid's hands were loose at his sides, and Tex had the start on him.

Tex's blunt gun muzzle was rising. Harris Evers, three paces behind Pryor, had a pistol out and raised, and he let go, firing past the Rio Kid. But he missed Tex, the slug striking Turkey Craw in the throat, killing him.

The roar of Evers' pistol startled Tex. The flash lighted the Avengers, with their blackened faces.

Two revolvers bellowed, within a few feet, muzzle to muzzle. The Rio Kid felt the air as Tex's missed his thigh by an inch. His own Colt, as he took that vital breath of time necessary to deadly aim, suddenly blared. A surprised glare came to Tex's eyes, disbelief, and his knees buckled. A moment later and Tex joined Turkey Craw on the walk.

The Rio Kid swung, running lightly back to the alley where their horses were held.

"Let's go, gents!"

To himself, as he rode off, he thought:

"A good night's work. We're whittlin' Smothers down to size."

Olsen had died before his trip to Washington. Turkey Craw, Marty, Popeyes and other lieutenants of the murderous Smothers' gang had fallen to the skill of the Avengers. Few of the gunmen would surrender. They feared the noose, and many had outlaw prices on their heads.

Tabor had delegated his authority to the Rio Kid, who thus represented the elements opposed to Smothers' criminal syndicate. And at the same time, the Rio Kid sought to save his friends whom he had brought to Leadville.

He was playing a most dangerous game, practically single-handed, against Smothers and all his killers. He had his plan worked out, and was sure it would succeed, sooner or later. Smothers must be driven to desperation, to a gamble which would place him in the power of the Rio Kid. The fight for the wealth of Leadville rose to furious pitch.

"And if what has happened tonight, after all that has gone before don't goad Smothers to desperation," mused the Rio Kid, "nothin' will!"

He was considering that the Avengers had been at their job for five days, during which they had accounted for fifteen gunnies, all known killers and members of Smothers' inner circle. Among the men on whom Smothers most depended had been Popeyes, Tex, Turkey Craw and the guards who had been caught at the flint rock.

Mireles, risking his neck to report to his General, as he called the Rio Kid, had told Pryor that Smothers was in the last stages of fury, and had offered ten thousand dollars for the smashing of the Avengers.

Careful not to injure innocent men, the Avengers had struck only at proved members of the outlaw ring, men who lived by the gun and would die by it rather than answer to the Law. . . .

The Mexican, meeting the Rio Kid the second night after they had killed Popeyes, reported that many of Smothers' strong-arm killers had quit. They had saddled their horses and fled from Leadville to escape the Avengers. More were threatening to go. They were in panic, well aware that the Avengers would mark them all, strike when they were not expecting it.

"Smothers'll have to act as soon as he sees the chance," decided Pryor.

To meet Celestino, the Rio Kid had climbed a high point from which he could command the country for many miles around. It was an Apache Indian trick, to get up above and thus have the advantage. He had stayed there after the Mexican had left, and noon had come and gone.

The Rio Kid, lying on a flat rock in the warmth of the sun, let his keen eyes roam over the broken country below. Suddenly he grew alert. He watched, fixing his vision to a point slightly to one side of the movement he had caught.

This time he glimpsed a man's figure. The fellow was leading a small burro, working through some huge, spewed boulders, and coming, slowly but surely, in the direction of the hidden camp.

"Huh!" he thought, "mebbe this is it!"

Like Smothers, the Rio Kid also was getting impatient. The people in the hidden canyon were suffering from exposure and insufficient nourishment. He wished to smash the criminal gang in Leadville and be on the move again.

It was not his way to let the grass grow under his feet. Tabor had entrusted him with a great mission, and he also had to save his friends of the wagon train.

Going back, he worked down to the grassy draw where Saber waited. Saddling up, the Rio Kid started toward where he had seen the man with the burro.

The dun gave him warning, for the wind was blowing toward them. Saber sniffed, rippled his black stripe, and the Rio Kid knew the mount had whiffed the donkey and the stranger. Dismounting, the Rio Kid went forward on foot and saw the intruder stooped over a deer trail down a rocky slope.

He did not recognize the man. The stranger was lean, clad in worn buckskin, with an old coonskin cap on a head of untrimmed light hair. He was examining the ground carefully, taking his time.

He might be a prospector, the Rio Kid thought. And never would he hurt a harmless person.

The fellow straightened up, unhooked a canteen from the nodding burro's pack, had a drink. He moved with sinewy power, and the Rio Kid who knew all there was to know about tracking and trailing saw that the buckskin-clad man was an expert.

Pryor stole back, mounted the dun, and trotted straight up the trail. He whistled shrilly, a tune of the day, so that the stranger would hear him.

As he broke out into view, he saw that the burro was out of sight. The man was staggering toward him. When he glimpsed the mounted Rio Kid, he raised an arm, weakly, and fell on his face.

Intrigued by this play, the Rio Kid approached, though ready for action. The fellow might be trying to draw him in, to kill him. He could see both hands, however, and they were empty. Getting down, he stooped beside the stranger.

"Water!" whispered the gaunt-faced, bearded man. He rolled his eyes. "I—I'm plumb done in, Mister!"

133

"Lemme give yuh a hand, pardner," the Rio Kid said softly, certain of what this fellow was, now.

He lifted him up, making sure that he had no hidden guns inside his buckskin shirt. The spy acted his part like a master, simulating a person starving and almost dead of thirst.

After a drink and a bit to eat, he explained:

"Lost my burro—he fell over a mounting. I ain't been through these parts afore. Was huntin' gold and silver. I'm shore obleeged to yuh for savin' my life. . . . Why, I don't even savvy yore name!"

"Make it the Rio Kid."

Under his dropped lashes, Pryor saw a swift, fierce light flash for an instant into the scout's pale-blue eyes.

"Rio Kid? Never heard of yuh. But I'll never forget now."

"S'pose yuh come back to camp with me. Yuh can fatten up and rest, and we'll lend yuh a horse."

"Yuh're a white man, Rio Kid!"

"What's yore handle? I'll want to interduce yuh to my friends."

"Fanner—Joe Fanner, from Santa Fé."

The Rio Kid put Fanner up in front of him and took him straight to the hidden camp. Hot food, more liquid, revived the gaunt scout. He shaved off the long beard stubble, the growth of many days.

Harris Evers drew the Rio Kid aside, that evening.

"I don't want to queston yuh, Rio Kid," Evers said, "but some of us are worried 'bout this Fanner hombre. S'pose he's a spy for Smothers?"

"He is," replied the Rio Kid, "but don't let it out, Evers. I'm goin' to use him. We'll turn him loose tomorrer."

Fanner slept in the camp. He was up early, and ate a hearty breakfast. He was profuse in his thanks to those who had helped him.

"I reckon I'm strong enough to ride right now," he

said tentatively to the Rio Kid. "I'd like to get back to New Mexico and home soon as I can."

"We'll lend yuh a mount."

Before noon, Fanner rode off, south, as though heading for New Mexico.

CHAPTER XVIII

Mass Attack

☐ When four days had passed, after Fanner left the hidden camp, the Rio Kid knew that big forces must be gathering because of the report carried to Leadville by the spy.

Trailing to Leadville himself, the Rio Kid once more met Mireles, who had proved so invaluable to him. Celestino reported that Fanner had been with Smothers and had given the killer chief the exact location of the enemies he wanted to crush. And Smothers had at once given orders to call out every fighter for an attack on the camp.

The Rio Kid had kept close watch, on his return to his friends, and at last, from the heights on the back-trail, he had seen the huge band of gunmen headed toward the hidden camp. He had at once dashed back to join his hard-bitten, grim-faced fighters.

"They're on their way, boys!" he reported.

The Rio Kid had made his arrangements for this. He had everything timed perfectly. He had himself forced this chance for a final showdown, and there must be no slip.

"Yuh reckon they'll come through this evenin'?" asked Johnny Burnett.

"I doubt it," replied Pryor. "Too hard work to get through these canyons in the dark. However, we'll be ready if they do, boys. Evers is watchin' on the trail."

Soon Evers came stealing up. There was, perhaps, but another hour of light before the night fell.

"They've pulled off the trail into Eagle Canyon," Evers reported. "Fanner and Smothers' gunny chief are comin' over the ridge on foot."

"Everybody outa sight," commanded Pryor.

Through the rocks, he glimpsed Fanner and a black-clad devil, one of Smothers' minions, as the spy and gunny took a long-distance peek at the camp which, following Pryor's instruction, was apparently unalarmed and preparing for bed.

The Rio Kid's followers were ready, but the great band of killers did not move again after dark.

It was not until the first gray mists of dawn rolled up, the canyons still deep-shadowed, that the word came they were approaching.

The way showed to Fanner by the Rio Kid was the only route feasible for horsemen. Great rocks hemmed in the trail, with the feeder brook on the left and more stones beyond.

Fanner and the fellow in black leather, at the head of their forces, came slowly into the narrows, feeling the way. Behind them the gunnies lined out, in small bunches, the column extending back for some distance.

Not a sign or sound gave warning that behind certain boulders, higher than the trail, the Rio Kid had set his men. Rifles, shotguns, Colts, were full-loaded.

The Rio Kid was down at the entrance end. He didn't want to spring it too soon. He had placed Evers at the camp exit, with strict orders not to let any gunnies past. And then, as two-thirds of them were in the trap and the morning light grew, shots rang out and sudden, shrill cries.

"Surrender, gunnies!" bawled the Rio Kid, his stentorian Army commander's voice booming in the cut.

But they would not give in so easily. Instead, guns began roaring at him.

The Rio Kid let loose with a shotgun, filled with buckshot. He lit a match, then, ducking down, he touched the flame to a fuse. Throwing himself on his face behind a granite spire, he heard the whoops and yells as the gunnies pressed forward to the kill.

A minute later a tremendous explosion rocked the universe, as smoke, dirt and broken rock rolled to the sky.

The rear-guard of the attackers was enveloped in this, and horses sprawled on the trail or fell over the steep bank into the brook, their riders stunned, shattered. A hail of rock fragments descended, and the Rio Kid, shaken in spite of his stout protection, pulled himself together and came to his knees.

As the smoke cleared, he saw that the explosion of mining powder he had skilfully set had succeeded in blocking the exit from the gorge.

"Throw down yore guns!" he shouted again.

Bullets snarled at him in reply, and his Colts went to work with their deadly speed. As the ringing in his ears subsided, he heard the fire of his friends above. From the high rocks hemming in the pass, the Avengers had opened up as the attackers sought to fight it out.

The Rio Kid could see the battle. The gunnies, slashed by the lead from the rocks, began to mill. The scattered, concealed miners made poor targets. Bullets flew thick, and the shouts of wounded mingled with the screaming of a wounded horse.

Evers, Burnett and fifteen fighters were ripping the van of Smothers' gunnies, throwing a stream of hot lead into Fanner and the chief of the attacking fighters. The two leaders went down among the first, and after a few ineffective shots, the van wheeled and tried to retreat. They pushed and fought in their effort to escape, but the main gang and the smashed rear guard blocked the way.

Panic struck, worse than bullets. A mad melée ensued, as cursing, frantic hired killers, nerve entirely gone, thought only of getting away. They used their guns on one another, and slashed in their madness at their comrades. Weaker ones fell under the hoofs of their comrades' animals.

As they crushed back, the Rio Kid's second line opened on their flank, cutting them down.

Over the canyon rose a red haze, as the sunlight touched the ridge.

"We surrender!" a quavering, fear-stricken gunny chief screamed.

The rest began throwing down their weapons. . . .

Smothers sat in his den that evening, awaiting the return of Fanner and "Black Pete" Rush, the men he had despatched to deal with the Rio Kid, Evers, Burnett and the rest of the real owners of the Potato Hole Mine.

Squirrel Hart was by his side. They were drinking.

"I feel better, Squirrel," Smothers growled. "I reckon this is the end. I told the boys to let none get away."

"How soon yuh s'pose they'll be back?" asked Hart.

"Oh, Fanner should send a messenger in before dawn, I guess. I'm tired of that Rio Kid sidewinder. I'll be glad to pay for his scalp. Black Pete said he'd bring it to me. And this'll cook the Avengers, too. I figger this is the last real fight I'll have in Leadville. I'll cook Tabor's goose next."

"The Avengers was the thing. The boys were quittin' wholesale," said Hart. "They had to be checked or we'd've been left alone, I believe—"

He stopped short, and both men lifted their heads, listening.

"Wonder who that is?"

"Mebbe it's Fanner come back!" cried Hart.

"It's mighty fast—"

Two gunnies were on guard just outside the hall door of the private room in the Giltedge. The portal stood half ajar, and Smothers, looking through, saw one eye turn toward the back of the hall.

"Hey!" shouted the sentry, and went for his gun.

He folded up an instant later, as two shots banged in the corridor. His mate quickly joined him.

Smothers leaped to his feet with a curse. He was standing up, a hand thrust into his coat pocket when the Rio Kid jumped over the quivering bodies of the guards and into the room.

"We're here, Smothers!" cried Pryor. "The Avengers! Yore gang's smashed! Yuh fell into my trap mighty neat, and—"

"Watch heem, General!"

Mireles spoke from the window. Crouched by the table, Squirrel Hart's hand had slipped to a gun at his hip, and he was hidden from the Rio Kid. In the lamplight, steel flashed, as the Mexican made his throw. The long knife drove into Hart's back, behind the heart. Squirrel flexed back, fell with a grunt at the feet of the man he had served.

Smothers knew the time had come to face the Rio Kid. The hand in his jacket pocket gripped a short-nosed revolver and he fired through the cloth at Pryor.

The Rio Kid's gun was up, but his eyes had been attracted for a breath by Hart's fall. He felt the slash of lead in his thigh, and then, with his feet spread and a smile on his reckless lips, the Rio Kid let his Army Colt speak.

Once was enough. Smothers caught the lead between his furious, flicking black eyes. He fell, hit the table, tipped it and rolled off to join Squirrel Hart.

The Rio Kid laughed. Then he keeled over, blood flowing from his side.

"I am back, Rio Kid," cried Horace Tabor, seizing Pryor's hand and pumping it.

The former mayor of Leadville had arrived, at last, in the Colorado mining center. He had finished his work in Washington, and was elated that Colorado would soon be a state.

The Rio Kid was somewhat drawn. The wound dealt him by Smothers had kept him abed for a long time and he was just up and able to ride again.

Tabor was profuse in his thanks.

"Yuh saved Leadville from the dirtiest polecat who ever walked, that Smothers hombre," he told the Rio Kid earnestly. "Incidentally, yuh got back the Last Chance for me. I understand Smothers was after my best properties and everything worth while in Leadville, and the way he was sailin' he'd have got 'em. Forgery, murder, thievin'—he was willin' to do 'em all. Fake papers, bribery, killin' put him in."

"That's all right, Tabor," drawled the Rio Kid. " 'Twas a pleasure to beat Smothers out. And I had to help those folks I led up here. Did yuh hear what happened to their mine?"

"Yeah. Too bad the Potato Hole petered out, after it looked so promisin'." Tabor nodded. "But that's the way it goes. Yuh never can tell with minin'."

"They're decent folks. I hate to see 'em in trouble."

"I savvy that, Rio Kid." Tabor's honest eyes were serious as he looked straight into the Rio Kid's. "I know yuh took their welfare to heart. They don't have to worry, either, not while Horace Tabor is around. Rio Kid, I done sold 'em the Last Chance. Traded it to 'em for the Potato Hole."

"That's mighty white of yuh, Tabor. I appreciate it."

Horace Tabor shook his hand. The Silver King of Leadville was at the peak of his power. His mines were paying, and he had every hope of soon going back to Washington as a member of the Senate. Fame had come to Tabor. His luck seemed never to run out.

And yet, as might a man climbing to the top of a steep mountain the precipice was just a step or two ahead. Tabor's luck was at its zenith, but it was soon to fall, never again to rise. But not before, the Rio Kid was always glad to remember, he had had his month in the Senate.

A step sounded outside and young Harris Evers entered the room. Dorothy was at his side. The girl smiled brilliantly at the Rio Kid, and came to him, taking his hand.

"We've just been married, Bob dear!" she cried. "I'm so happy!"

"Congratulations!" boomed Tabor, shaking hands heartily. "The party's on me! Evers, I've just traded the Last Chance for yore Potato Hole. Yuh'll have plenty to take care of yore bride."

Evers' eyes lighted. Dorothy plucked at his sleeve. She stopped smiling, looking anxiously at her husband.

"Well—I've quit minin', Tabor," Evers said. "I got a new job buildin' the Santa Fé up through the Royal Gorge. Engineerin'."

That was what Dorothy wanted and Evers had surrendered to her wishes.

"She's right," thought the Rio Kid. "This minin' game is madness. They'll get on fine and Evers'll be a lot better off with regular work to do. He'll be a fine railroader."

The Rio Kid had cleared Leadville of its criminal killers. His job there was done.

Soon he rode out of Leadville, with his faithful mate, Celestino Mireles. The Danger Trail called to him.

He glanced back at the smoke rising from the smelters, at the mining town roaring high in the Rockies. They were headed for the Royal Gorge and thence the plains of Kansas.

Life rolled on, and so did the Rio Kid. Restless of spirit, his urge for adventure kept him moving along the vast Frontier, guns ever ready to defend the weak and helpless, those in need.

Tom Curry was born in Hartford, Connecticut and graduated from college with a degree in chemical engineering. Leo Margulies, editorial director for N. L. Pines's Standard Magazines, encouraged Tom to write Western stories. In 1936, Margulies launched a new magazine titled *Texas Rangers*. Leslie Scott wrote the first several of these 45,000-word novelettes about Texas Ranger Jim Hatfield, known as the Lone Wolf, published under the house name Jackson Cole. Tom Curry's first Jim Hatfield story was "Death Rides the Rio" in *Texas Rangers* (3/37) and over the succeeding years he contributed over fifty Hatfield tales to this magazine alone. Curry also wrote three of the series novelettes for *Masked Rider Western* and some for *Range Riders Western*. It was in 1938 that Margulies asked Curry to devise a new Western hero for a pulp magazine and Tom came up with Bob Pryor. *The Rio Kid Western* published its first issue in October 1939. Subsequently Curry expanded several of his Rio Kid stories to form novels, published by Arcadia House, with the hero's name changed from Bob Pryor to Captain Mesquite. Possibly Curry's best Western fiction came during the decade of the 1940s, especially in the Jim Hatfield stories and in his Rio Kid novelettes. After Margulies was released from Standard Magazines, Curry quit writing and began a new career in 1951 with Door-Oliver, Inc., that lasted for fourteen years, working in their research and testing laboratory in Westport as accountant, purchasing agent, and customer service representative, making use at last of his chemical engineering degree. When Curry retired from Door-Oliver, he resumed writing Westerns sporadically for Tower Books and Pyramid Books and, later still, for Leisure Books. In October 1969, Margulies informed Curry that he was to be publishing a new digest-sized publication to be titled *Zane Grey Western Magazine* and he wanted Tom to write some new stories to appear in its pages featuring a number of Zane Grey's best known characters. These stories would be published under the house name Romer Zane Grey. Curry put a lot of talent and energy into so many of his Western novelettes, particularly the Rio Kid adventures, and his stories can still intrigue and entertain.